Cockingt

Charlie

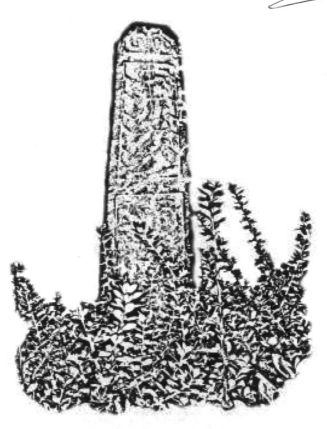

**'Then let it be so...
...that which is written.'**

elmore

Published by **elmore** 2008

ISBN 978-1-869986-02-5

Charlie Shields
Babbacombe
Torquay

www.carypark.co.uk

elmore

For my sister
Elizabeth

1957 - 2007

Chapter One

Saturday had arrived, and Jason should have felt at least some excitement as he lay under his duvet, anticipating the day ahead. However, he'd already been told of the arrangements, and they didn't include hanging around the shops in Exeter with his friends. They didn't even involve staying at home to watch telly or to play games on his PC. Then, for the third time in five minutes, he heard his mother's shrill voice rising from the bottom of the stairway and recalled the previous week's conversation.

'Your father wants you to stay with him this weekend.'

'But I hate Torquay; it's boring.' These had been his only words of protest and, as usual, they went unheeded.

'Sorry, but he insisted. Anyway, I've already made plans to go shopping in London with some friends.'

The sixteen-year-old had been the victim of this *sudden-change-of-plan* scenario on many occasions, but he grudgingly accepted that being batted between Exeter and Torquay was standard practice since his parents' separation two years before.

'But it's not all bad news, Jason. Your father's taking you to a midsummer festival. Now, what a nice way to spend your birthday, don't you think?'

Jason had detected a hint of sarcasm in her tone and knew that this was a pathetic attempt at making *herself* feel better. For him, however, things were going from bad to worse. And as he gazed at his bedroom window, the steady drizzle sweeping into the glass summed up how he was feeling about things. What a great start to the weekend this was...*not*.

A smile then briefly appeared on his lips. Perhaps, with a bit of luck, the stupid festival might be rained off, in which case he could do something else a bit more interesting. Or the whole thing might even be one of his dad's crazy jokes – like last month's sponsored tree-hugging event that turned out to be an exciting trip to Woodland Adventure Park.

Eventually, after finding the energy to dress with yesterday's strewn clothing, Jason went downstairs into the kitchen where his mum was noisily rummaging around.

'Now, where did I put the damned thing?' she said, then turning to her son. 'Oh, you're up at last. Have you seen my train ticket anywhere?'

Jason allowed her to rake through a couple of drawers before lazily saying: 'It's in your bag; that's where you put it last night.'

'Oh, right. So where's that?'

The teenager shook his head and watched her scuttle through to the lounge, only to return a few seconds later.

'Okay, Jason. Don't forget to pack a few things for yourself. And you'd better hurry; your father will be here shortly.'

He sighed. 'Oh, come on. It's not like I'm going for a week or anything.'

'Still, make sure you take clean underwear for tomorrow, and let's hope your father's on time; my train leaves in an hour,' before once again going through the kitchen drawers. 'I'm sure I saw my mobile phone somewhere in here...'

Jason groaned and opened the fridge to fetch some orange juice. Then, sitting at the table, he flicked through the television channels and sipped at his breakfast.

Half an hour later he sauntered into the lounge to find his mum at the window, looking anxiously at her watch.

'I told him to be here at half-past ten,' she said. 'He's already two minutes late.'

'Don't worry. You know what he's like.' Jason was well aware of how unreliable his dad could be. He hadn't come across any other father who had never worked – at least not in any *real* sense, and only vaguely remembered that he did a bit of gardening. Also, his mum had told him about his so-called band – Dad and one of his long-haired cronies called Steve – who would perform at the occasional folk festival. But not *proper* work, and never enough to ensure that he and mum were financially supported in any way.

With that, there came from outside a *phut-phut-phut* followed by a loud bang. He looked through the bay window to see a car pull up; only, it appeared more like a multi-coloured sewing machine on three wheels, and his dad had been driving this embarrassing heap as long as Jason could remember.

'I just hope no one sees me getting into that thing,' he said to his mum, who had already opened the front door.

Going into the hallway to join her, Jason heard: 'Where the hell have you been? You know I've got a train to catch.' He then watched his dad walk down the steps from the pavement.

The man's hair and straggly beard, both now almost totally grey, hung longer than ever, but the large golden hoops swinging from his ears hadn't changed in years. And as he ambled closer, hands in the pockets of his brown waistcoat, it seemed that the harsh words had passed straight over his head.

'And good morrow to you, too.' Jason's dad grinned all the way to the doorway. 'Sorry, but the car wouldn't start. Bit of damp, I think, from this drizzle.'

'A *car*? Is that what you call it?' blasted his estranged wife. 'Time you got yourself something decent, if you ask me.'

Jason knew that his dad wouldn't rise to the challenge, and sure enough the bearded figure was soon looking into his son's brown eyes.

'Happy birthday,' Dad beamed. 'And how's my little Jaz today?'

'He's not a *little* anything,' came the sharp response. 'He's a young man, in case you haven't noticed.'

Jason didn't mind the term of endearment. More than that, he liked it, and despite the threat of a three-wheeled ride to Torquay he returned a smile, followed by a brief hug.

'Come on, you two. I've got my train to catch.' Jason's mum was standing on the garden path, hands on hips, glaring at father and son together in the hallway.

A few seconds later she closed the door and gave her son a quick kiss on the cheek. 'I'll phone you tomorrow night when I get home,' were her last words just before she sped off in her soft-top to make the short journey to the local railway station.

Jason's dad was soon turning the ignition key in his own car, only to produce a muffled splutter and a plume of black smoke from the rusting exhaust. 'Told you she's a bit damp. Give us a push, will you, Jaz?'

Ten minutes into the half-hour journey Jason had heard enough from the panpipes bellowing out from the car's radio cassette. He switched it off and turned to his dad.

'So this thing you told Mum we're going to...tell me it's just made up, and that we're really going to the moors or something.'

'Sorry, Jaz...it's for real.'

Jason folded his arms and stared straight ahead with face scowling, as his dad told him about the festival in the village of Cockington on the outskirts of Torquay.

'What are you talking about?' The teenager sounded unimpressed.

'It's the summer solstice, Jaz…midsummer. Have you never heard of it?'

He thought for a long moment. 'Well, kinda. There was something on the news this morning about these people at Stonehenge…all dancing around the stones when the sun came up. Is that what they do at this Cockington place, as well?'

'I don't think so, son. And as far as I know it's the first time there's ever been a festival held there.'

Jason shook his head. 'All this solstice stuff is weird if you ask me. I mean…it's like Mum says…have they nothing better to do with their time than to prance around some silly stones at stupid o'clock in the morning?'

Checking the mirrors, Dad offered his response. 'There's more to it than you could ever imagine, Jaz. And today's event is even more special.'

'Oh, yeah.' Jason's tone remained scathing. 'So how's that?'

'Because there's a blood moon tonight.'

'*A what?*'

'A lunar eclipse. It's when the full moon is swallowed up by the earth's shadow, turning an eerie deep orange colour. We can stay up to watch it if you like.'

'But what's the big deal?'

'You just don't get it, son, do you? The summer solstice *and* a blood moon all in one day? That only happens every couple of hundred years or so, and it means we're entering a time of profound change.'

Jason groaned. 'Why do you believe in all this New Age rubbish? Mum told me you've got crazy ideas about the universe and stuff like that.'

His dad sighed. 'And just what would your mother know about the cosmos? As far as I recall she spends all her time running up credit cards in the High Street shops.' He then looked his son in the eye. 'Not my idea of meaningful existence.'

Jason considered what he'd heard – and it sounded about right. But hold on...didn't *he* himself have all the latest trendy gear? And weren't his mp3 player and mobile phone more expensive than those of anyone else?

'Material goods aren't everything,' Dad went on. 'It's making a difference that matters, and believing that any positive action from you can benefit other beings on this planet. I hope one day you'll realise that.'

Jason grunted and stared at the passing hedgerows. He simply wasn't in the mood for a lecture from a grown-up. Especially from one that was so rarely around.

The sun greeted Jason for the first time that day as they drove along Torquay seafront. Burning through the low cloud, it placed the distant town of Brixham under its brilliant spotlight.

'I was hoping it would chuck it down, so as this stupid festival would be cancelled,' he said.

His dad laughed. 'As bad as that, is it?'

'Yeah, because it sounds like it's gonna be full of freaks. And there's no way you'd ever catch me dancing around stones in the ground…even if they *were* there.'

Dad's only visible response was a prolonged wide grin.

A couple of minutes later they turned into Cockington Lane, leaving the busy tourist resort behind them. Dense woodland either side of the narrow road soon changed day into twilight, and Jason rolled down the window to sample the cool air.

'Look, red squirrels on that tree over there,' he said, appearing surprised.

'You'll see a lot of them here.' Dad explained that the forests around Cockington were some of the last locations in England where these creatures could be found.

Jason quietly surveyed the leafy scene for a few more moments and, with a developing frown, enquired: 'Have I been here before?'

Dad shuffled on his seat for a moment. 'Er…I don't think so.' He then looked at the intense pensive appearance on his son's face. 'Anyway, just a few more minutes along this lane and we'll be there.'

As they approached the village the woods yielded to increasingly open countryside, and Jason noticed a small winding stream on the right. Some ducks splashed through the water, but which sort he didn't know.

'Mallards, they are, Jaz. The colourful one's the male, and the brown one the female.'

Jason grumbled. '*Huh.* Think I don't know that?'

Continuing to look through the window, he became aware of the increasing numbers of people milling around the lanes and footpaths. Some on their own, a few couples, and several small groups. And, apart from a few men with ridiculous beards and trailing robes, they all seemed to be quite normal.

'See, Jaz. Not a freak show after all.' Dad reached into the back of the car and produced what appeared to be a type of cowboy hat, with a white feather stuck to its side.

Jason watched wide-mouthed as his father placed the hat onto his greying head. 'Tell me you're not gonna wear that thing.'

His dad looked bemused. 'I take it you don't like my fedora?'

Jason was unsmiling. 'It's the most *uncool* thing I've ever seen...apart from your car. And if anyone asks, I don't know you, *okay*?'

With that, the car turned off to the right before coming to a spluttering rest in a narrow dirt track.

'All right, Jaz. Pick up what you need and let's explore.' Dad placed a camera into his canvas haversack.

Jason sensed the enthusiasm in his father's voice but couldn't raise the energy to match it. 'Yeah, it should take all of five minutes to check out the whole place.' He then brought out his mobile phone from his backpack and groaned. 'Typical. No signal.'

'I promise, Jaz, you won't be needing that here. And you can leave that music thing behind as well.'

'*No way*, they're staying with me. Can we just go now and get this over with?' Jason pushed open the car's door against the tangle of brambles at the side of the track and stepped out. He then zipped up his cotton jacket and placed the hood over his short spiky hair.

'Is that really necessary, Jaz?'

'Yeah, it's well cool. Not like that thing on your head.'

'Each to his own, I suppose.' Dad straightened the feather on his fedora. 'Anyway, let's follow the masses and see what's brewing.'

Chapter Two

Just as they reached the centre of the small thatched village, a white horse pulling an open-top carriage came to a juddery halt in the road immediately in front of them.

'*Whoa, Georgie Boy, whoa!*' cried the coachman, pulling hard on the reins.

Jumping back a little, the teenager saw that the man's silver hair fell onto his shoulders and that he wore a hat similar to his dad's. And while Jason was gazing at the feathered headwear, the character spun around to address him.

'You be going to the Keeper's cottage then, lad?'

'*Me?* Oh...I'm not in the queue.'

'*Get on.* There be none.'

With a quizzical look on his face Jason turned to his dad, as though looking for guidance.

'Go on, Jaz. You can't leave Cockington without taking one of its famous carriage rides.'

Jason briefly considered the offer before shaking his head and looking back to the coachman. 'Maybe next time, mate.'

As the horse clattered off along the road, Jason's attention turned to the village map displayed on the crumbling stone wall just behind him. He noticed a large red dot, and next to it some bold type: **YOU ARE**

HERE. With his finger he followed one of the public footpaths, then paused.   'Cockington Manor...does anyone live there?'

Dad nodded. 'The owner's a bit of a recluse, but they say that today's festival was his idea.'

As Jason frowned, his eye caught the grey shaded region to the rear of the manor house. It looped around to occupy a large part of the surrounding countryside and included the notice: **NO PUBLIC ACCESS - STRICTLY PRIVATE**. He then slid his finger a little lower and asked his dad about the green coloured area to the front of the house.

'That's a cricket field. And it's also where most of the action should be.   Come on...time to sample the atmosphere.'

From where he'd been standing, Jason had already become aware of a faint mix of musical notes dancing merrily through the warm air, and as he walked past an inn and under a chestnut tree towards a boardwalk, he was able to distinguish some of the individual instruments. A guitar, a whistle, a fiddle, and some type of strange piano were all in there for sure.

Within a minute he felt the warm sun strike his face from the almost blue sky, and he found himself at the edge of a large clearing.

'What do you think, *now*, Jaz?'

For the first time in a long time, Jason struggled to offer an opinion. '*Wow!*' was just about all that he could find.

Lowering his hood, he marvelled at the sights in front of him. He felt as if he'd just entered a massive stadium; the towering trees on three of the sides providing the grandstands, and the large building at the far side completing the arena. That just *had* to be Cockington Manor, he reasoned; and sure enough, there stood the cricket pavilion on the slope to the right.

'There must be thousands of people here,' Jason eventually managed to mutter. 'Can I walk around for a bit?'

'No problem, Jaz. Have you got enough money to spend, by the way?' Dad removed a mound of loose change from a pocket on his orange coloured jeans.

'*Huh*. You can keep the shrapnel.' Jason delved into his own pocket and, as well as a few pound coins, flaunted some paper notes. 'Mum gave me thirty quid for my birthday.' He smirked and then checked the time on his mobile phone.

'Okay, Dad. See you in about an hour outside that big house.' Jason, now feeling the heat and unzipping his jacket, waited for his dad's nod of approval before he ambled off and melted into the summery crowd.

Soon he was feasting upon vegeburger and chips from one of the stalls. This fast-food wasn't what he was used to from Exeter High Street, but it beat the other weird stuff that was on offer – like organic wild rice with forest mushroom, and melted goat's cheese with wholemeal panini.

As he continued to saunter through the swarming masses and around the various displays, he saw for himself that this was indeed a special event. In one of the presentations he stood mesmerised as a middle-aged character demonstrated a few paper engineering skills. He'd often wondered how they managed to build pop-ups into children's books – and now he knew the basics for himself.

Next stop was a tent where a gypsy-like young lady was selling what she claimed to be precious stones. But not just your ordinary type – she insisted that these ones resonated at a particular frequency, which could interact with a person's biorhythms via Uranus. Jason had never heard so much rubbish in all his life, yet it brought a smile to his face.

Moving along, he casually tossed his spent food carton to the grass, before reaching his first live musician – some old looking character with a shaved head, large white moustache, and dark round glasses. The poster suspended from his keyboard advertised the performer as 'Dizzy', and Jason began to understand why as he watched the man guzzle freely from a bottle of wine on a table next to him.

After this he listened to someone deliver a talk on creative writing, but the hour soon sped past and the time came to meet up with Dad. Trudging towards the front of the manor, he saw him already sitting down on the grassy bank, reading a book.

He looked up to Jason. 'Enjoying yourself?'

'It's alright, I suppose.'

'Seen anything you like?'

'Some of it's okay, but there's some funny people here.'

Dad raised his eyebrows. 'Different from you, you mean.'

Jason sat down. 'No...just *well* weird, but I wouldn't mind another look at some of the things.' He noticed a wry smile appear on his dad's face.

Following a brief rest, Jason looked towards the two great pillars standing like sentries at the front entrance of the manor. 'That looks really old, Dad. When was it built?'

'Hundreds of years ago, I suppose, just like everything else around here.'

Jason saw that the huge wooden door was ajar. 'Can we have a look inside?'

Dad looked uncertain. 'I don't really think we're allowed,' he said, before glancing around and grinning. 'But then again...no one's looking.'

Within a few seconds they were in, and the first thing to strike Jason was the imposing stained-glass window straight ahead at the far side of a long corridor. It seemed to stretch from about head height right up to the high ceiling, and it was almost as wide. Vibrant blues, greens, and yellows made up most of the scene, with bright red crosses placed in each of the four corners.

For a long moment he looked at the depiction of a woodland setting, which included youthful humanlike figures, some of whom had wings. Next to catch his eye was the large bolted door situated directly under the ornate window and next to the bottom of a spiral stairway. 'I wonder where that goes,' he said aloud, but really to himself.

'I don't know, Jaz. And by the size of that padlock, we're not going to find out. Come on, let's go back and rejoin the fun.'

A few seconds later they strolled back through the clearing, stopping every now and again to watch some Morris dancing, listen to music, or to browse the stalls. And whilst Jason was fingering indifferently through a box of second-hand books, he was interrupted.

'You like reading?'

'What...?' Jason didn't recognise the man now standing next to him. He looked a lot older than his dad and had a long white beard, with pigtails sprouting from the back of his thinning hair.

'I see you're looking at fantasy books. Do you like them?'

Jason took a step back from him and looked to the 'Celtic Legends' section. 'I don't read a lot, but my dad does... he's just over there.'

The stranger squinted over. 'Ah, yes. I see he has good taste.'

Jason hesitated for a moment before saying: 'And what about you...do you like books?' He noticed the man's brilliant white robe, decorated with a splashing of silver stars and crescent moons.

'Yes, I do.' The man smiled. 'And my favourite is one that was written a long time ago.'

'*Really?*'

'Yes, that's right. An enchanting story of the little people and their fight for survival.'

'You mean a fairy tale?' Jason glanced away and saw that his dad had started to walk towards him. Then once again turning to face the stranger. 'That sounds like a good sto...'

'What's wrong, Jaz? You look like you've seen a ghost.'

Only after a long moment was Jason able to speak. 'That man...the one who was here...he just...'

Dad glanced around the busy stalls. 'What man's that?'

Jason provided a garbled description of the character that had just vanished. He then looked vacantly to his dad and grabbed his arm. 'I'm *not* making this up or anything.'

'I'm sure you're not, Jaz.' Dad gently released his son's grip. 'But that's what happens at festivals. Perfect strangers talk to you and then, before you know it, they're off with someone else.'

Jason thought for a moment. 'Well, there was something funny about him...about his eyes...like I'd seen him before.'

Dad shook his head. 'I wouldn't worry about it, Jaz. Sounds like one of the druids making conversation, that's all.' He then looked to his watch. 'Now, I'm famished. Fancy a bite in the inn?'

'No, thanks. I've already had something. You go on...I want to look at that map again to see what else there is to do about here.'

'Okay, Jaz. You come and get me when you're ready.'

They walked back over the boardwalk towards the village centre, before going their separate ways.

Having not drunk anything since breakfast, Jason now felt in need of some refreshment, and as he reached the main road he was pleased to see a sign hanging from a pink building: **Weaver's Cottage – Tea Shoppe and Souvenirs**. Looking up, he saw a tidy thatched roof with pale blue flowers cascading from the pots on the narrow window sills.

Lowering his head to avoid the roses on the trellised doorway, Jason stepped into the shady but cosy interior, where it seemed that he was the only person there. Four or five small tables filled the snug room, and in the fireplace stood a spinning wheel. To his right he saw a small doorway, which he supposed was the way through to the kitchen, and so he ambled over to have a look.

The place still seemed deserted, and the aroma of home baking almost lifted him off his feet and through the door. He was still savouring the moment and just about to strike the little brass call bell that hung to his left, when he was startled by a soft voice from behind.

'Good day, young man.'

Jason spun round to see a woman sitting at one of the tables.

'And how can I help you?' she went on.

'Oh, er, just a can of orange, please.'

The chair screeched against the slabbed floor as the figure pushed herself up and walked towards a wooden counter, onto the side of which she placed her hands, as if feeling her way around. Her white hair protruded from a headscarf, though looking at her face she seemed to Jason just a bit older looking than his mum. However, as she had brushed past him, he noticed that she barely came up to his waist.

'Have you seen the Keeper's place?' The woman was groping around inside a nearby cupboard.

'*What?*'

'The Keeper's cottage…have you been there?'

'Er, no…well, not yet.' As Jason stroked his chin he saw a large cross swaying from the end of a chain around her neck. The dull grey metal was decorated with bright red stones and featured a circle at its centre.

She soon produced a can of cola. 'Is this what you wanted?'

Jason frowned. 'No…but it'll do.' He held out a ten-pound note to pay for the drink. 'How much is that?'

The woman smiled. ''Tis free for you.'

'*Free?* But why?'

Her hazy blue eyes only just managed to clear the counter, and she seemed to focus beyond Jason to the wall behind. 'It doesn't matter. Just mind your step now…don't want you falling or anything.'

Looking down to his trainers, Jason saw that one of his laces was trailing onto the floor, and so he bent over to tuck it back in.

'Thanks,' he said on standing up, 'But how…?' Jason peered into the kitchen just in time to see the figure merge with the darkness. He was rooted to the spot, still staring into the shadows, when he heard some loud clopping from outside the door.

After stooping once more on his way out, he saw that a horse and carriage had parked just down from the tea room, directly across the road from the village map. The same man held the reins, but this time there sat someone next to him. A smaller person – maybe a child, Jason reckoned, with a green hood raised over their head.

'Ready, then?' the coachman swivelled round and called out.

Jason had a quick glance about, but seemingly the man was talking to him. '*Me?*' He placed a hand to his chest.

'I don't sees no one else.'

Jason hesitated for a few seconds, then walked slowly over to the rear of the carriage. 'Ready for what, exactly?'

'The Keeper's place.' The man was grinning. 'You *did* want to see it.'

The teenager slowly nodded. 'Okay…supposing I do. What's so special about it?'

From his seat the coachman leaned closer and spoke softly. ''Tis where magic do happen, my friend.'

'Huh...you sound just like my dad.'

'Your father be wise, then.'

Jason had a long drink from his can, followed by a stifled burp. 'So how long is it there and back?'

'About as long as it takes for one of they pub lunches and a pint of ale.'

Without really thinking of what he'd just heard, Jason produced a ten-pound note to pay for the ride.

The coachman shook his head. ''Tis on me, lad. I can't change that muckle thing you got.'

Jason wasn't going to argue over yet another freebie. After crushing his empty can in his hand, he drop kicked it into a nearby bush and promptly climbed into the shiny leather seat in the back of the old wooden carriage.

Chapter Three

The hooded figures sat near the lakeside, their heads peering over the blanket of buttercups that separated them from the bushes at the far side of a thatched cottage.

'I sense a powerful presence close by,' said the girl, shutting her eyes and holding a hand to the side of her head. 'Come on, Tusher…let's be gone.'

'Don't be daft, Ethera,' replied her male companion. 'The Keeper's not been around these parts since the day you was born. And anyway, just a little longer and us'll be feasting on they lovely goosegogs.' Tusher led her by the hand, all the while keeping a keen eye on the red sandstone building up ahead.

For a short time he harvested the soft fruit from the prickly stems, before Ethera suddenly clutched his arm.

'What were that?' she asked, nervously.

Tusher spun around, a bewildered look on his face. 'I hears nothing.'

'That noise…'twere the Keeper's door.' The girl tugged forcefully at the boy's sleeve. 'And a giant approaches, I tell you.'

After a short delay Tusher sighed. 'So be it, lass.' He slipped his hand into Ethera's. 'Let's to yonder copse go and hide in there. '

With the hoods still over their heads, they scurried into the dense undergrowth.

Jason spent most of the ten-minute journey attempting to play the tourist and show an interest in the picturesque surroundings. However, he had become fascinated with the music arriving from the front of the open carriage, recognising the tune as one of his favourites.

'Just gimme respect, man. You know what I mean, Bro.

I ain't no sucker, no sucker for you, no...'

The coachman, and not his seemingly younger companion, sang several verses, but he kept returning to these same lyrics. Jason found it quite amusing that someone as old as this should be indulging in modern hip hop.

After coming to a halt, the man pointed to the side of the tarmac lane. ''Tis only a hundred yards through that gate, and if you're lucky there'll be a carriage waiting here for your return.' He then jumped down and went to attend to the horse.

Jason stepped off and turned to the coachman who was now stretching up to pat the horse's neck. 'Okay...thanks for the ride. I won't be long.'

'Aye, but just watch your feet, lad. Them woods be trickier than you think.'

These words of advice had already been forgotten as Jason approached a narrow archway, which was set into a towering stone wall that ran either side as far as the eye could see. He noticed a half-opened rusting barrier at the entrance and quickly read the warning on the small hand-painted plate: **Strictly Private – No Public Access**.

Jason glanced back to the coachman, pointed to the sign, and shrugged his shoulders.

'Never mind, lad...'tis old. Just you get on up that track.'

On passing through the portal, the climate seemed to change, prompting Jason to zip up his jacket. The shade from the creaking trees seemed denser than anything he'd experienced before, and squinting upwards he saw only a few patches of blue between the looming parasols. The drifting shafts of sunlight that did manage to pierce the thick canopy shone like milky beams onto the forest floor, highlighting in their wake the darting hoverflies and other flying insects.

As he edged slowly through the knee-high vegetation, it seemed that other beasts were also busy – even though he couldn't see any. There came rustling from the ferns on a bank to the left, flapping in the holly to the right, chirping from somewhere behind, and a loud rat-a-tat-tat from a tree trunk high above.

Jason quickly realised that it wasn't the carefully managed woodland of a leisure park with its mix of tarmac and chipped-bark trails; this was strewn with the skeletons of ancient trees, some still standing and crooked, with others fallen and at peace within the undergrowth.

Eventually, he reached a narrow trampled path, but there was still no sign of the cottage, even though he reckoned that he must be at least halfway there. A little further on, as he walked around a bend, Jason came across what appeared like a large duck pond. Its banks consisted mostly of rugged rocks and clumps of rhododendron, the trailing leaves of which teased the glacial surface of the dark water.

Then, rejoining the trail and walking behind a large thicket, there it stood – only a stone's throw across a smaller pool of reddish murk. And even though the cottage appeared creepy, Jason somehow felt himself drawn closer.

Other than the disparate sounds of the wildlife, he felt alone and began to wonder why, with the cottage seemingly so special, no one else was around. Was this the right place? Jason then glanced at the time on his mobile phone: **13.53**, and decided on just ten more minutes to check things out. And surely, even his dad would be pleased with the efforts he'd made to show such an interest.

Now almost within touching distance, the cottage was a patchwork of green and red with all the moss and algae clinging to the crumbling walls. The old building looked derelict, and Jason deliberated over moving any closer for fear of being clobbered by falling masonry. Lifting his head upwards, he also determined that the thatched roof hadn't been replaced in years, if at all. It was nothing like the postcard perfect one that he'd seen at

Weaver's Cottage – this was patchy and loose, with ferns, moss and weeds making permanent homes over half of its decomposing surface. Below the thatch and along the eaves ran a slatted wooden area, into which a tangled mass of ivy had invaded. And the building's front windows appeared to have been boarded up, but on closer inspection Jason could see that the battered covers were the rotted remains of old shutters.

Soon he found himself standing on the few worn granite steps that led to a panelled front door. It had no letterbox, number, or name attached, but it did have a handle. Jason was just about to grasp the large metal ring when he paused. His attention had been attracted to the small orange and brown butterfly flitting just over his head, and in so doing he saw some other markings, this time carved into the weathered stonework above the entrance. Small fronds obscured some of the lettering, but Jason still managed to see: **GA EK EP R**, and was now certain that he was at the right place. Feeling pleased with himself, he grasped the handle and gingerly swung open the squeaking door.

Jason had only just stepped one training shoe inside the building, when he was on the receiving end of a blinding white flash. With hands then raised to his aching eyes, his first thought was that someone had used a camera with a turbo-charged flash.

'Okay…who's there? Is that you, Dad?' he managed to stutter.

There was no reply, and only when his eyesight had recovered could he see any detail. The small windows now allowed free passage to the forest daylight, and Jason wondered at the warm glow that filled the room. He saw what looked like several burning oil lamps dotted around, and became aware of a pleasant aroma of cooking hanging in the atmosphere. 'Is anyone here?' he then called out.

Apart from the remote cawing of crows from outside, he received only an eerie nothingness in return. So once again he tried, now louder, and his voice now possessed a slight tremor.

'Look, this is so not funny.' Again the silence returned; this time cold, dark, expectant, and Jason felt his senses sharpen. Nevertheless, he felt compelled to give the place the once over.

The wooden floor creaked as he walked cautiously towards the fireplace, where he cried out again. 'I know you're in here somewhere.'

As he waited for a response, he caught sight of a large wooden chair at the side of the hearth. Soon running his hands over its dark surface, Jason found that a variety of winged figures had been carved into the wood – all the way from the base of its legs to the top of its arching back.

Next to this chair there stood a small table, upon which sat a wooden bowl and cup, alongside a small loaf of bread and a jug of water. This table *hadn't* been set for two, Jason decided.

The crackling logs in the fireplace tossed orange flames up to the base of a small cauldron that was suspended on a metal bar. Jason thought it strange that he hadn't seen any smoke rising from the chimney outside but, nonetheless, this just had to be origin of the mouth-watering smell, and so he went to have a closer look. After grasping the ladle from the mantelpiece, he stirred the simmering contents of the pan, only to discover some kind of thick vegetable soup. Jason wasn't hungry, yet the thought of sampling the delicious looking mixture did cross his mind.

Then, as he replaced the ladle, he heard soft shuffling sounds from the top of a rickety staircase at the other side of the fireplace, as though someone was walking on a dusty floor but couldn't be bothered to lift their feet.

'Who...who is it?' As Jason peered nervously upwards he could almost feel his hair stand on end.

Once more, no answer was the reply – and his skin prickled. Eventually, as he plucked up the courage to move towards the bottom step, the shuffles abruptly stopped, and a croaky voice descended.

'I bid you welcome, my friend.'

Jason took a deep breath and was in two minds about going any further.

''Tis alright, lad. Come forth.'

The voice sounded friendly enough and so, step by creaky step, Jason slowly climbed the stairs.

'Over here,' he next heard.

Jason stared into the near-blackness of the far corner of the room. His eyes strained to catch anything in the poor light, but very gradually a soft white glow began to emanate from the gloom – a small, shimmering cloud to begin with, before a more defined and larger shape emerged.

Soon he found himself facing the radiant figure of a man standing in the corner, dressed in a brown robe with orange sleeves. The character had long grey hair just like some of the strange folk that he'd seen that day but, unlike that Druid figure, this one's garment had no embellishments.

Even from across the room Jason could see that some things weren't quite right. 'You gotta be kidding.' He moved a bit closer to the stranger who seemed about chest high to himself. 'My dad's put you up to this…those pointed ears and funny eyes…some sort of birthday surprise, *yeah*?'

'Come by here, lad.' The old man waved Jason over. 'Feel with your own hands.'

After a brief hesitation, Jason placed his shaking fingers against one of the misshapen organs. The surface felt just like skin, and warm, too. It was even a bit flaky with some small but prominent blood vessels. And now he was also able to see those weird eyes more closely – one was red and the other green.

'Okay.' Jason briefly raised his hands. 'This is nuts…what's going on?'

'Do not fret so.' The old figure held in his hand a crooked staff with an angelic creature carved into the top. 'But shouldn't I be the one asking such things?'

'What do you mean?'

'My friend, how would *you* feel if you did find a stranger in your abode?'

After a moment Jason slowly nodded. 'So *you're* the gamekeeper.'

The man laughed a little. 'If you say so.'

'Well, that's what it says above the door.'

'*Does it?* And do you believe everything you see?'

'Hmph. Course not.'

'And what about magic, my friend? Do you believe in that?'

Jason sniggered. 'No way, and I think it's time I was going.'

The man slowly lifted his staff high above his head. 'Then let it be so…that which is written,' he said, before crashing its base into the floorboards, shrouding himself in a cloud of sparkling dust.

Jason laughed nervously as he looked at the glistening figure. 'I get it now. You're a wizard, and you're gonna put a spell on me. Tell you what…the ears are very good…I'll give you that…and the contact lenses…nearly had me fooled, they did. When I see my dad I'll ask him how he managed it.'

With that, he turned around to go down the stairs, and reaching the top step, he looked back. 'And one more thing, *Merlin*. Nice trick with the camera…' However, all that was left to see was a shrinking and shimmering white cloud. Jason then shook his head and shouted into the near-gloom. 'Yeah, nice wind-up, mate.'

A moment later he was once again standing on the doorstep of the cottage. And after slamming the door behind him, he couldn't wait to give his dad a hard time.

Chapter Four

The great beast thundered over the clearing, its power ably controlled through the taut reins. Approaching the nearby manor, the gallop was reduced to a trot, and the girl waved to the man standing alongside the imposing entrance.

A minute later he took her by the hand and assisted her to dismount onto the cobbles. 'Megan, my dear. You know that it's dangerous and not becoming of a young lady to ride as you do.'

Stroking the animal's strong neck, she looked pleased with herself. 'Yes, I know...but it's more exciting that way.'

The man then clicked his fingers towards the stables at the side of the house. 'Move yourself.' His voice was raised. 'I do *not* provide cider and shelter for you to idle around.'

The stable lad was cowering as he quickly made his way over to the front of the building. 'Aye, My Lord...sorry, My Lord.' He barely had the courage to raise his head, it seemed, as he took hold of the leather straps with his shaking hand, before guiding the horse over to the stable door.

'And give him a good grooming, you useless imbecile.' A spray of the man's spittle landed on one of the girl's rosy cheeks, and the tone changed. 'I'm so sorry, my darling. Please, allow me.' He produced a handkerchief.

Reaching into the frilled cuff of her velvet sleeve, the girl retrieved her own. '*Please*, Father. Let *me* do it.' She took a few seconds to dab her face, before being asked how the horse had performed.

Megan nodded. 'Fast as the wind, but a little jumpy, I fear...especially through the woods.'

Her father raised his eyebrows. 'Please tell me that you didn't stray into the combe.'

Megan then sighed. 'Why do you worry so?'

The man placed a gentle hand on his daughter's cheek. 'It is perilous there, and I only fear you may...'

'...be gobbled up by the evil wood sprites?' The girl had opened her eyes widely as she finished the sentence.

However, her father remained straight-faced. 'I wouldn't be so flippant, my darling. You know what happened in there, and we've all heard the fearsome beasts for ourselves, howling from the depths of the forest.'

Megan moved in closer and embraced him. 'If it makes you feel better, I promise that I ventured nowhere near the combe. Now, if you will excuse me...' She then stood by one of the tall pillars that guarded the entrance to the manor. 'I must remove these awful muddied boots.'

Just across the yard the stable lad was bolting the door behind him. In so doing, he looked across the musty interior to his grinning companion, who was leaning against the enclosure. ''Tisn't funny, Beckford. Cockington's getting worse…I feared he'd have my head then.'

'Oh, get on, Ball, my old mucker. He be the same now as the day his good lady died.'

'Aye, but why do he take it out on us so bad?'

'Easy.' Beckford slid off the gate. 'Because there be no other poor beggars round these parts to bellow at.'

Ball thought for a long moment. 'You'm right, mate. 'Tis just a wonder he lets young Megan ride them horses at all.'

'Aye.' Beckford moved to refill his drinking cup from the scrumpy barrel. 'God help us all if anything befell her.'

From the steps of the cottage Jason scratched his head and looked towards the lake set amongst the shrubs. Was it as wide as that before? He couldn't be certain. In fact, he wasn't even sure if he should be able to see any water from his position outside the old building.

Jason then looked down to the rough ground and searched for the track that would lead him back under the arch, yet all he saw was a narrow flattened trail in a waist-high sea of stinging nettles, which meandered off in the opposite direction. Now beginning to feel a bit confused, he decided to move towards the lake – and from there, find a way out. And so, after pulling down his cuffs to protect his hands, he headed off.

This was no duck pond, after all. The breeze that had begun to pick up blew across a stretch of rippling water that was at least three times the size of the one that he'd stopped at before, and on this occasion Jason could find no clumps of rhododendron that he'd seen cloaking the water's edge on his way towards the cottage. Instead, as he felt the goosebumps rise on his skin, he saw that the small lake was populated with beds of tall reeds.

Then, beyond the far side of the waterway, he noticed some movement amongst the trees. Just a glimpse, but it looked to him like two small children holding hands – both with their hoods up – disappearing into the shadows.

As Jason continued to scan the woodland for any further activity, he detected a muffled combination of knocking and wailing sounds descending from above – as if produced by some unearthly orchestra. The haunting notes ebbed and flowed with no regular rhythm, and as the breeze eased off, the strange music climbed back into the high foliage.

Pushing his increasing anxiety to one side, Jason inhaled deeply and tried once again to retrace his steps. And surely, on the right and down the hill a little way there would be a track that leads to the gateway. So that's where he went; or at least, where he attempted to go.

Jason's return journey wasn't as straightforward as he'd imagined, and the intimate company of briars ensured only slow and painful progress. He found that he was stamping a virgin track through the thick undergrowth; the prickly walls rising high either side making it virtually impossible for him to see where he was going.

For how long he'd picked his way through this hostile obstacle course, Jason didn't know; and it was a tired and bedraggled figure that eventually collapsed into a clear pathway. However, any feeling of relief was short-lived. Recognising the large boulder in amongst the brambles, Jason now realised that he had only succeeded in creating his own natural maze – from which there seemed to be no escape.

It was time to stay calm. Everything was *cool*...really. Nothing to worry about. Another deep breath...and slowly out. And in...and out. Okay, maybe it wasn't a wind-up; the scratches and the pain were all too real...but hold on. What did the coachman say about the Keeper's place? Was it something about magic happening there? *Yeah*, that was it, and even though he struggled with the very notion, Jason had no option but to go along with it. And if something magical *was* going on, could it be undone? Perhaps if he were to go back to the cottage and speak nicely to that mad wizard, he could sort things out.

Cool, man, cool...there's the boulder. Now, it's just a case of standing on top and finding that decrepit old building...

Some time later, as Jason slid down from his elevated position, he felt a bead of sweat rolling down his cheek.

As far as his eye could see there was nothing but trees, trees, and more stupid trees. There wasn't even any sign of the lake, let alone the cottage, and in this moment he was wishing that he'd joined his dad for lunch.

Then an idea. What if...and why not? He'd done the same thing at the adventure park the month before when looking for his dad.

Not too far away he saw a large conifer and, with renewed vigour and the help of a half-rotted stick, crashed through the brambles like a jungle explorer to stand breathless at its large bole. Then, looking to the ground, he noticed a few gooseberries scattered around and, just for a moment, wondered how they could possibly have arrived there.

Squinting upwards, the trunk seemed impossibly high. Nonetheless, Jason placed his zipper and backpack on the soft cushion of dried pine needles at the base of the tree, and he jumped up to grasp the lowest branch with his hands. After heaving himself upwards, he was able to gain a proper foothold and continue his ascent.

Bough by slow bough Jason rose into the canopy – every now and then surveying around for familiar landmarks. Hand up, tight hold, and pull. Foot up, firm grip, and push. Jason was gasping as he reached a level in the tree that was way above most of the other growth in the wood, and so he stopped for a rest.

Casting his eye one way, it was more of the same; except this time he was looking down onto the treetops. Then, peering through the branches in the opposite direction, a smile came to his face. Down on the left, in the distance, he noticed a vast opening in the middle of an extensive forest. There was movement there, too, and Jason steadied himself against the trunk to look again. Speeding over the turf he could see a white horse, and the rider, dressed in green…was that a girl with long blonde hair?

Even though he thought it was too far away for him to shout for help, Jason could still detect the rumble of the pounding hooves as the animal raced towards a large house at the far side of the open space. And at last, here was something that he'd seen before – a door, with the pillars either side.

Okay, so now he knew roughly where he was and in which direction to move. Nothing magic was going on, after all – he'd simply got himself lost. Except, where were the browsing masses and the countless stalls? Right, so the festival must have finished and, that being the case, Jason reasoned that a worried Dad would be scouring Cockington, desperately trying to find him. Then again, he might be standing at the bar drinking his fourth pint of beer, debating how the capitalist system was destroying the planet.

As Jason looked down to place his foot on a sturdy limb, he saw that the lace on his training shoe was hanging loose once again. However, given his position, he couldn't do anything about it this time, and just as he went to move his hand onto the next branch, Jason was forced to an abrupt halt. If he could have rubbed his eyes he would have done so, but all that he managed was to turn away for a moment and look back.

Yet there *was* no mistake, and he tried to imagine how they could possibly have got up there. Huddled towards the end of the bough, with a cluster of pine cones just above their blonde heads, was what looked like two small children. The hoods on their green shawls were lowered, revealing shoulder length hair, and four bare and dirty feet stuck out from the bottoms of ragged grey trousers.

Jason couldn't help but gape, taking in their chalk white skin, striking blue eyes...*and* their pointed ears. 'Okay, you must be the elves, and this is your forest, yeah?' His own voice may have had a quiver, but to Jason these two creatures looked absolutely petrified – just like a pair of quaking garden gnomes. 'Shouldn't you be sitting on a toadstool or something, instead of up here?' He was trying his best to speak in a friendly manner, and eventually it seemed to do the trick.

'Dumni...us be Dumni.' The shaky voice was that of a boy, and he didn't take his eye off Jason for one moment – not even to blink.

'Well, *Dumni*. I've seen enough magic for one day.' Just as Jason went to continue his downward journey, he peered over once again to the little people. 'But if you know the way to the Keeper's cottage, that would be a great help.' He gave them a few moments, but he received only fearful silence in return.

Jason had seen it all now, and moving steadily back down the trunk he remembered the precise words of the coachman. *''Tis where magic do happen, my friend.'* Not kidding there, mate. And if he saw him again he'd be asking a few questions. Also, what was it the gamekeeper said? Something like, *'Let it be so...'* What was all that about?

If he hadn't been so absorbed in his jumbled-up thoughts, Jason may have given more attention to the dangling lace from his training shoe. He never did notice it snagging around a small notch, and it was enough for him to lose his balance as he neared the base of the tree.

Plunging backwards, Jason caught the startled look in the faces of the little people high above, before the passing greenery moved as if in slow motion. Down and down and down – slowly sinking through the breeze – and not wishing it to end. Pleasant, comforting thoughts came to mind, filling him with an inner calm that he'd never sampled before, each just a brief snapshot from his younger days. Like the time his dad brought a puppy home for him when he was just a toddler, his first day at school when he scraped his knee on the playground concrete, and the family holiday in France when a crab pinched his big toe on the beach. Down and slowly down, not wanting it to end, hoping it wouldn't, yet knowing all the while that the darkness awaited him...

Jason lay on the soft forest floor, revelling in the enchanting chorus of birds and insects. Feeling so comfortable, he could have remained there for ever, and only when his perfect peace was disturbed by a sustained overhead flapping, did an earthly reality began to kick in – along with the pain in his head and lower leg. Then eventually delving deep to find the energy from somewhere, he managed to open his eyes to the looming conifer and, piece by piece, began to recollect the events of the day.

The last thing that he remembered was seeing a couple of elves high in the tree…and then nothing. How he came to be lying on the ground he didn't quite know and, after feeling his matted hair and checking his blood-stained fingers, Jason simply guessed that he must have fallen. However, did he really find little people in the tree? Was it just a dream, and was every strange occurrence of this day part of that same experience? Perhaps, if he closed his eyes again, he would wake up in his own bed.

The soft crackling that emerged from the adjacent vegetation soon distracted Jason from his innermost thoughts. For a long moment he watched and waited, but could see no movement. Then the increasing pain, radiating from his left ankle up to his thigh, began to make him feel queasy. It was time to get going, he decided – but couldn't. The leg wouldn't budge, and Jason began to sweat.

His backpack lay just beyond his quivering fingers. If only he could get his phone out from it, he could call for an ambulance. No good – and the more he tried to reach over, the more he felt like someone was pumping broken glass the wrong way through his entire body.

Calm down, Jaz. Just calm down. Deep breath in…and slowly out. And for a short time everything *was* cool again, until Jason very gingerly lifted the frayed bottom of his jeans. He had never seen his foot sit at such an angle compared to the rest of his leg – little wonder he was in such agony. Then another deep breath before raising his jeans a little further. Briefly, Jason felt like he was going to pass out, but instead he lapsed into tears and cried out for help as loudly as his suffering would permit.

A long moment later the only creatures to answer his call confirmed that he hadn't been dreaming, after all. Now flat on his back, with mouth ajar and face contorted, Jason held out a despairing hand to the elves as they hesitantly emerged from the briars, the girl just behind the boy.

'Please…help me. I…I can't…can't move.' A mixture of blood, sweat, and tears trickled down Jason's temple. He then listened to the elves as they began to argue with one another.

'Oh no, you don't Tusher. Can't you see he suffers enough?'

'No matter, lass. I says us finish him off – good and proper – and put him out of his misery. Then tell the elders that us did slay a giant.'

As Tusher cautiously closed in, Jason caught a glimpse of the mossy rock that the elf was now holding up to his chest with both hands. His heart missed a beat, then pounded. 'No…please…I mean you no harm.'

Now only a few paces away from his defenceless target, Tusher raised his hands high in preparation for the strike.

'*No*, I tell you.' Ethera's shout was loud enough to startle a couple of wood pigeons roosting high in the conifer.

Even her companion jumped, before shouting back. 'And why not?'

''Tis only a boy. That's why.'

'Aye…but a giant all the same.'

'And a good one…I feel it in my bones. So put that thing down.'

Jason was listening closely and held out his hand once more, this time pleading softly. 'Please…help me…my leg's broken…and I can't get up.' He then witnessed the little people confer once again.

'He ails bad, Tusher…I must help.'

The elf boy eventually sighed. 'Oh, all right.' He tossed the rock back into the long grass. 'The giant might not have fangs like they say, but get too near and he'll eat you, for sure.'

'Well, that doesn't bother me…but his pain does.' Ethera began to edge closer.

As Jason attempted to speak to them again, he was taken by the girl's comforting voice.

'Husht, now, husht.' She had her finger up to her lips, and a few steps later was kneeling next to Jason's pallid face.

Her skin shone as brightly as the petals of the daisy that lay tucked behind her ear, and just staring into her eyes and sensing her cool hand on his brow provided Jason with some welcome respite from his agony. He saw something distant in her gaze, *and* something intimate – as though she could feel what he was going through.

Ethera then softly stroked Jason's cheek, and with each tender movement of her delicate fingers a wave of relaxation rippled through his tortured body.

'How came you here, Giant?' she asked, eyes now closed, as if her mind had drifted elsewhere.

With the girl's help, Jason had now regained some of his poise. 'I was at the Keeper's place, then couldn't find my way back to the track.'

'What track be that?' Tusher's voice was full of mistrust.

'The one that brought me here…to the cottage.'

As Ethera continued to apply her caring touch, Tusher spoke again. 'So what business did you have there?'

Jason described what had happened to him in the cottage and told them of the old figure that had appeared.

'That sounds like Bora…Bora Macool. He's the Keeper of the Dell.' Ethera frowned, then edged towards Jason's feet. 'And he only turns up when there's something big going on.'

'Aye...you can say that again,' said Tusher, sounding sarcastic.

Now feeling more comfortable, Jason was able to push himself up a little, so as to rest back on his elbows. He then watched as the elf girl daintily raised the bottom of his jeans and examined the buckled limb.

'Oh, my dear boy.' Ethera carefully replaced the trouser leg and looked to her companion. 'We need white willow. And water, too. Now go...with haste.'

Tusher shook his head and pointed to the helpless Jason. 'I'm not leaving you here with him.'

But he received a terse response. 'Just do as I say.'

Soon the elf boy had returned and went to hand over a few small lengths of silvery green bark, before hesitating. 'Be you sure about this?' He was still looking suspiciously at Jason.

Ethera grappled with her companion's arm and snatched the woody pieces from him. 'Well, he isn't going to eat me now.' Then turning to Jason. 'First, have a drink, and then chew on this here bark. It tastes of witch's brew, but it quiets the hurt.'

Very slowly, Jason raised a hand and accepted the coarse lumps from the elf. And as he did so, he noticed a metal bracelet around her wrist, studded with bright red stones.

'Go on,' the girl continued, 'then I'll do something about your poorly leg and head.'

Jason managed a few welcome sips of cold water from the wooden cup that Ethera held to his dry lips, then popped a morsel of bark into his mouth. It was hard, but not crunchy, and he'd only just started chomping when the bitterest taste filled his mouth, making him wince.

'It'll do you good.' Ethera began to caress his cheek once again.

Jason soon found that she was right. The foul taste eventually disappeared, along with all the pain that had filled his head and leg. Smiling with sheer relief, he looked to Ethera who had begun to manipulate the fractured limb, and as much as she handled it, and moved it, and twisted it, Jason felt next to nothing.

'Wow,' he said. 'This is really good stuff you gave me.'

'There be more to it than that,' said Tusher. 'Just you see.'

Within a short time Ethera was tending to the large bruise and cut to Jason's head. It felt to him like she was massaging the injury, and this time he found the experience quite pleasurable.

A little while later the girl said: ''Tis done...you can stand up now.'

'You what?' Jason's mouth was left gaping.

'She said you can get up.' Tusher was now standing with a stick in his hand. 'But no foolery, mind.'

Jason shook his head. 'I'm not going to hurt you. I just want to get back to my dad.' He then pulled up his blood-stained trouser leg to find no sign of injury – not even a mark on his skin where once a jagged bone had protruded. His head, too; the huge bump had vanished, along with the deep gash.   He looked to Ethera. 'That bark stuff I can understand. My dad's always talking about things like that, but what about the rest? How did you do it?'

Ethera blushed. 'Just a talent I found out I had when I were little.'

'Well, it's a miracle, if you ask me. And, er…thanks.' Jason stood up and walked unsteadily over to the conifer to rest against its trunk.

'You never did tell us why you was here,' said Tusher, who had since thrown his stick into the long grass, 'and us don't even know if you have a name.'

Jason introduced himself, and the elves sat on the pine needles as he gave an account of the Cockington festival and of his visit to the Keeper's cottage. He finished with the events that had lead him to climb the tree.

'…and so you see, I can't really remember the fall. But what I do know is that I have to get back to the inn to meet my dad.'

'Some of what you say don't sound right,' said Tusher, frowning. ''Tis a strange world…this Cockington place.'

Jason laughed. 'Tell me about it. It's not every day I get to meet miracle-working pixies.'

Ethera then spoke. 'You say you did see the Keeper. We can show you the way back to his cot, if you want.'

'Thought you were never going to ask.' Jason smiled and now walked steadily over to the little people. 'Can we go now…because it looks like it'll be dark soon?' He picked up his zipper and backpack from the base of the tree.

'He be right, Ethera. The light fades and the gloaming be nigh.'

Weaving through the rough vegetation and onto a rocky track, Jason discovered for the first time the true size of his saviours. Tusher, wielding a twisted stick, reached to around his waist, and Ethera just a little lower. However, despite having the height of young children, they had the faces and features of teenagers – together with a peppering of spots. And looking to their tiny hands and bare feet, Jason was amazed to find that their skin appeared completely unscathed – even after they had trampled over a thick blanket of brambles.

'So Jason,' said Ethera, once again holding Tusher's hand, 'this festival you speak of, it sounds akin to the Feast of Belenos.'

'And what's that?' Jason continued to walk just behind them.

''Tis when the Sun God awakens and breathes new life into the world,' Ethera went on. 'And it happens at the time of the shortest night.'

Jason chuckled. 'And I suppose you dance around stones in the ground, as well.'

His off-the-cuff statement brought his two companions to an abrupt halt, and both had a stern look about them as they turned around.

Jason also stopped and began to feel uneasy. 'Was it something I said?'

Tusher frowned. 'How do *you* know of the Great Circle?'

After a moment's thought, Jason recalled the news report from Stonehenge that he'd seen that morning and assumed that was what the elf was talking about. 'Oh, yeah…well, I've never been there myself, but my dad has.'

'Now you be havering,' continued Tusher, shaking his head.

'*What?*' Jason had a vacant look on his face.

'I means you be talking silly. Because no giant has ever cast eyes upon the sacred stones. And as for that midsummer thingy you did speak of…' Tusher produced a loud sigh.

'What do you mean?' Jason went on.

'Belenos be six moons away…it ain't yet come to pass. So how can you have your feast this very day?'

Jason was left scratching his chin and, as he did so, the elves continued on their way, muttering.

'Right nasty bump on the head that were,' said Tusher to Ethera. 'He not be thinking straight.'

By the time that they reached a wide stretch of water – one that Jason vaguely recognised – the first of the evening stars had begun to twinkle in the pale green sky.

'That be the Keeper's place yonder.' Tusher pointed into the near-blackness beyond the opposite bank. 'Now go, and best you never return to these here parts.'

'And why's that?' asked Jason.

49

'Because you giants is not welcome in our lands,' continued Tusher, 'and I cannot say what may pass if others of the tribe do find you here.'

Jason held his hands out at his sides. 'But surely you can see that I'm not a threat to you.'

'He is right,' Ethera said to Tusher, who still sounded unconvinced.

'Aye, but where there be one, there be many. 'Tis what the others do say. Now, *go.*'

Jason realised that any further debate would be pointless, and so he thanked them again for all that they had done for him. However, as he did so, there was a rustle of activity in the nearby undergrowth.

Tusher quickly held out his arms, preventing any further progress along the lakeside track. He looked to Ethera, and whispered: 'What say you?'

She stared blankly into the thick vegetation. 'Aye, I hear it alright, and I know that smell, too.'

'Well, stand with him back there, lass,' Tusher continued, 'and hold your husht. This one be mine.'

The elf boy crept forward a short way and looked to a large stone at the side of the path. Then grunting and using both hands, he managed to heave the dirty rock up to his chest and, after a final short gasp, above his head. And there he waited with arms swaying precariously under the strain.

After a long moment a slender muzzle emerged from the long grass, closely followed by a red and white coat, and finally a bushy tail. On sighting Tusher, the animal came to a standstill, staring directly at him with its hungry eyes.

'Come on, then. Come to Tush.' The elf displayed no outward signs of fear as the hackled beast crept menacingly towards him. 'Good boy. Just a bit more…I've got a little something for you.'

With that, a large projectile whizzed past Tusher's ear, travelling quickly enough for his hair to be ruffled in the resulting draught. And the wobbling rock that he'd held high over his head crashed onto the rubbly track, only just missing his feet.

However, one thing that didn't miss was Jason's backpack. It had already smacked the beast full in the face, prompting it to scamper off into the woods at high speed.

The loud yelp was still ringing in Jason's ears when a scowling and stomping Tusher turned to face him.

'You daft galoot…you had no right to meddle.'

Jason was taken aback by the elf boy's reactions. 'Sorry…but I was only trying to help.'

Tusher's cheeks were still red. 'Well, us don't need your help for anything. And as for old Foxy, I can take care of him on my own.' The elf pointed into the shadows. 'Now, be on your way.'

Jason was stunned into silence. Surely that fox would have mauled Tusher to death, so why should the elf be so ungrateful?

Going to pick up his bag, Jason took a moment to retrieve some of the contents that had spilled out onto the track. He then gave a final glance to Ethera's smiling face before moving off in the direction of the cottage.

He would probably have lost his way again if it wasn't for a flickering yellow patch of light up ahead. Realising that this could be the lower window of a lamplit building, he was filled with a sense of relief. And even though the trail underfoot was now unseen, he was soon standing on the Keeper's doorstep.

Turning the metal handle, Jason stepped onto the uneven floorboards. This was the same cottage, for sure. It may have been dark outside and almost unrecognisable, but he hadn't forgotten the lush smell from the simmering cauldron.

He closed the door and moved a few steps into the room. 'Okay, old man…you've had your laugh. Let me get back to my dad. *Now!*'

The place remained eerily silent, and Jason's tone mellowed a little.

'Look, Bora…that's your real name, isn't it? My dad's gonna be worried sick, and I bet the police are out looking for me. So you better let me get back to him.' Still no answer – and then he remembered. Perhaps now there would be a signal, and maybe he could phone for help.

But just as he began to rummage around in his backpack, a voice descended from above.

'Ah…the wanderer returns, I see. And looking just a bit raggedy from his day in the forest.'

Jason's attention switched to the top of the wooden staircase. In contrast to the welcome light in the room where he was standing, the upstairs chamber sat in darkness.

The first thing to emerge from the gloom was the flowing hem of a brown robe, followed a tasselled cord tied around his waist, and finally the smiling face of the Keeper, still holding his crook.

'You be wasting your time there, lad,' he said.

Looking to the screen on his mobile, Jason saw that there was still no signal. And not only that – the digital clock was displaying more or less the same time as it had done on his first visit to the cottage: **13.56**.

'That's right, my friend. Your father is only now sitting down to eat. And 'twill be just so as long as you remain in this world.'

'But…' Jason stuttered.

Bora raised his hand. 'This here broth were made for you, and we shall speak again after you have eaten.'

Jason was so hungry that he didn't need a second invitation. Therefore, when the steaming pot above the glowing embers called him over, he simply obeyed. He had no idea what the recipe was – but he didn't care. And with the bread and water still waiting on the table, a famished and thirsty sixteen year-old couldn't have asked for more.

Eagerly lifting the bowl from the table, Jason filled it to the brim using the ladle that he'd left on the mantelpiece. He was soon sitting on the wooden chair, dipping his crusty loaf into the rich soup, and wiping the drooling juice from his chin with his grubby zipper sleeve. Now, this *did* beat the fast-food on Exeter High Street – no sweat – and there and then he decided that this was the best food that he'd *ever* tasted.

After having his fill, Jason wiped off his face and had a long drink of water from his cup. Only then was he ready to speak. 'So what's this all about?'

The man shuffled over to Jason and sat on a chair next to him, his knees creaking in the process. 'Following our lives' paths…you and me both.'

Jason looked at him oddly. 'What do you mean by that?'

Bora grinned. 'It is for you to discover your own destiny, my friend. And as for me, I was fated to open the doorway into our world.'

'So where's that, then? *Nightmareland?*'

The Keeper shook his head. 'Far from it. This is the Great Dell…where the last of the Dumni do dwell.'

'Oh, yeah…Tusher and Ethera mentioned that name.' Jason went on to explain what had happened to him.

Bora now nodded. 'Always knew one day the maid would use her gift.'

'What's that, then?'

'You tell me, Jason. You felt it yourself.'

The teenager abruptly stood up, sounding almost aggressive. 'Okay, how do you know my name? And don't say I told you before, because I didn't.'

Bora remained seated and spoke calmly. 'I know all that comes to pass.'

'*Oh, yeah.* And how's that?'

'Because I exist within time…not across it.'

'*What?*' It seemed to Jason that the man was talking in riddles.

'Let me put it so.' Bora scored the end of his crook across the dusty wooden floor, leaving behind a straight line. 'That, my friend, is how *you* see time.'

Jason sat gaping as, once more, Bora scraped his stick over the bare timber.

'And this, how it is for me.' On this occasion he produced a large circle.

The teenager had a long hard look at the floor illustrations. 'Sorry, mate. But see all this hippy stuff…I can't get my head round it.'

The Keeper proceeded to use his staff as a pointer on the floor. 'Behold, the straight line has a beginning, a middle, and an end. This is your world – birth and life, before the finality of death. Then moving his stick to the circle. 'Here there is no beginning…and no end. No birth…and no death. That is my domain.'

Jason mulled things over for a long moment. 'Are you trying to say that you've always existed, and that you'll live for ever more?'

'If you say so, my friend.'

'A bit like a god, then?'

'If it pleases you to think that.'

'So where does this *gamekeeper* stuff come from?'

Bora grinned. 'Don't be fooled by what you see.'

'*Meaning?*'

'In other days I have been a simple tin miner on Dartmoor, and closer to your own time I assume the guise of a humble gardener.' Bora pushed himself up from the seat and lifted one of the lamps from the table. 'Walk with me. There is something you should see.'

Jason followed closely behind as Bora opened the door to the cottage.

'Come by here to the outside step, my lad.'

As Jason stood next to the Keeper, the man raised the flickering light to the stonework over the door.

'Tell me what you see *now*,' he said.

This time Jason pushed the ferns to the side, enabling him to reveal all the lettering.

'*Wow!*' He stared with amazement into Bora's creased face, then looked back to the overhead carvings which now spelled out: **GATEKEEPER**.

They both retreated into the cottage and sat close to the fading warmth of the hearth's glowing embers.

'Okay, Bora. If you can't say why I'm really here, at least tell me what comes next.'

The Keeper shook his head. 'I'm afraid you must find your own path.'

Jason groaned. 'But surely, you can tell me something.'

Following a moment's deliberation, Bora nodded. 'I've already told you of the Dumni, and I shall only add that this is how they were many years before your time.

And when you leave this cottage at dawn, keep to the beaten track.'

A frown then slowly appeared on Jason's face. 'Thanks for the dinner, mate, but I won't be here in the morning.' He then picked up his backpack, opened the front door, and stood on the top step. However, looking ahead into the blackness of the forest, Jason could only just about see beyond his nose, and the only signs that there existed anything beyond the cottage were the shimmering stars and the distant screech of an owl. Slowly turning around, he looked to Bora and spoke in a softer voice. 'Look, I need to get back to my dad...please.'

The Keeper gave a prolonged shake of his head, and his words were measured. 'I'm afraid that your only way back is to be successful in your quest. And just remember what I said about your father at that inn; you shall not be missed.'

Jason pondered for a long moment. 'Are you saying that I'm stuck here until I complete some sort of task?'

Bora nodded, but he remained silent.

Jason then slung his bag to the dusty floor. 'Well, that's just great, isn't it? A secret mission in Elfland and a dad who knows nothing about it. *Brill.*' He protested for a little while longer, but to no avail.

And so eventually, after accepting that the Keeper was not about to move on the issue, Jason couldn't hold back on a huge yawn, and his vision began to blur.

'"Tis best that you rest now, I feel.' Bora showed Jason to a bed of straw in the corner of the room. 'Sleep well, for trying times lie ahead.'

Very soon Jason had slumped onto his dusty mattress. He had many more questions for the Gatekeeper and wondered what would happen if he were unable to succeed in his quest. However, with his mind in a swirl and his eyelids feeling like lead weights, he decided to wait until the morning.

Chapter Five

The early morning mist hung like a ghostly cloak over the damp ground, as the two tribal elders reached the monolith at the centre of the Great Circle.

Clutching the ornate metal cross around his neck, one of the men cast his eyes over the runes; the greyness of the stone matching the tone of his voice.

'Lus, my friend, the message does not change. Yet, as much as I hope for better times, my heart is filled with dread.'

'Come now, Mans. 'Twould be no good for the others to hear such speak. The said day is five moons distant, and that which is foretold may yet come to pass.'

'Aye...only five moons and still no sign of Bora.'

On hearing the name, Lus groaned. 'That feckless oaf. His kind of sorcery cannot be trusted; that we know from past misdoings.'

Mans nodded and looked to the inscriptions one more time. 'Fool or no, the Stone of Celest foretells that the Keeper shall be the one to bring the boy to us before this coming Belenos.'

'And if a young giant does so appear, how shall we know for certain that he is the chosen one, and not just more of Bora's worthless trickery?'

Mans placed a hand on Lus's shoulder. 'By his deeds alone – nothing else.'

Jason discovered that he was alone in the cottage when he woke up, and his unanswered questions would have to wait until later. Initially, he thought to look for a fridge to fetch some orange juice, before realising where he was – and when. Then helping himself from the table, he had to be satisfied with a breakfast of bread and strong cheese.

Soon afterwards, as he went to open the door, Jason hesitated. He'd never been too fussy about wearing fresh clothing every day, but one quick look at the state of what he still had on was enough. The legs on his frayed jeans were blood-stained, as was his zipper, which was also riddled with snags from his encounters with the brambles. Delving into his backpack, he quickly changed into another hooded top and a fresh pair of jeans and socks. He briefly thought about his underwear, but they'd be good for at least another couple of days, he reckoned.

The sun was only just beginning to clear the treeline as Jason stood on the steps of the cottage, with the dawn chorus cheering the cool air. He looked above the door just to confirm what he'd been shown the previous night, and the letters were still there, standing out boldly in the morning light. He also noticed that the cottage wasn't so derelict – the thatch seemed fresher and the stonework more or less intact.

'Keep to the beaten track,' the Gatekeeper had told him, and after the previous day's unfortunate events

Jason had already decided to follow the instruction to the letter.

The first trail that he found was the one that he'd created himself the night before on his way from the lakeside to the cottage, and soon he was standing at the water's edge gathering his thoughts.

So what was he to do now? Come on, Jaz. Think, think, think – and then an idea. This was Dad's freaky sort of world, so what would *he* do? For a long moment Jason allowed his mind to merge with the sparkling surface of the clear water, waiting for a moment of paternal inspiration, until a voice told him: *'Remember to find your own path.'*

Jason jumped a little, yet as he looked around he hadn't really expected to see anything but a few shrubs ruffling in the breeze; Bora's words having stemmed from within his head.

'Keep to the beaten track...Find your own path...Keep to the beaten track...Find your own path...' He found himself repeating the words over and over, and only after a sustained moment of thought, did it dawn on him that this wasn't a contradiction in terms.

Then, just as he was contemplating his next move, the ghostly wailing that had filled the forest the day before once again descended from the treetops on the far side of the lake. It was also roughly in that direction that he had first come across the elves, and he decided to head over.

Remaining firmly within the established trails of trampled nettles and flattened grass, Jason neared the dense growth of woodland. The gentle wind then eased and, as it did so, the wailing faded back into the foliage, as it had done before. Just what *was* this sound, he asked himself, and with it now gone again, how was he to discover its source?

Determined to find the answer, Jason penetrated deeper and deeper into the forest, which became a shade darker with every step. At least there were no more nettles or other nasties to deal with now, and between the pillars of trees the soft humus underfoot made him feel like he was walking on air. Soon, however, as Jason ran his eyes up a steep root-ridden bank to a rocky shelf, there arrived a different sound form. This one had a definite beat to it – like wood on wood – as if someone was using a tree trunk as a drum, with a jungle type of rhythm that he quite liked.

Nearing the ledge, the tapping became more intense, and it seemed like the music was coming from the other side of the bank. Something else that Jason recognised was part of a song – along with the strangest of American accents. This shouldn't be, he reasoned. Not in this world or time.

After quietly heaving himself safely onto the plateau, he peered down to the narrow glade and found the cause of the commotion. There he saw an elf boy, complete with earphones plugged in, rapping and singing with the aid of an mp3 player. And next to him on the fungus infested tree trunk sat Ethera, tugging gently at his sleeve.

'Come on, Tusher,' she said. 'Enough of your larking about.'

Without looking, he pushed her hand away and continued singing.

'Just gimme respect, man. You know what I mean, Bro.

I ain't no sucker, no sucker for you, no...'

This was beyond Jason's belief. Just how did they get their hands on that? He was still coming to terms with the entertainment below, when Ethera suddenly turned her head to his position. She smiled warmly, but said nothing. In return, Jason placed a finger to his lips.

Tusher, with eyes closed and head bobbing around, seemed too pre-occupied to notice as Jason slowly made his way down to the elves, before sitting next to Ethera on the prostrate log.

Only at the end of the track did the elf boy open his eyes. Jason caught the look of surprise on his little face, just before Tusher pitched backwards over the trunk onto the grass, leaving his dirty bare feet in the air.

With the piece of modern technology still in his hand and the earphones now trailing on the rough turf, it was a red-faced figure that eventually pulled himself upright.

'I did tell you never to return here,' fumed the woodlander.

Jason grinned and performed a short breakdance, whilst singing the same lyrics that he'd heard from Tusher.

The elf was rendered wide-eyed and speechless by the dance movements, whilst Ethera clapped her hands wildly.

'That little black box were on the track where you did throw your sack at Foxy,' she said after the performance. 'How came the voices inside?'

Jason grimaced and tried his best to offer as simple an explanation as possible, but Tusher didn't sound convinced.

''Tis witchery. And why do you so linger in the forest?'

Inviting Tusher to take a seat on the log, Jason told them of his latest meeting with Bora.

'...so you see, I can't leave your world until I do whatever it is I have to.'

''Tis twaddle,' said Tusher, glowering. 'And why should us believe the ranting of old Bora after what he did do to you, Ethera?'

Jason looked puzzled. 'What do you mean by that?'

'*Hmph!*' Tusher went on. 'You can't even follow your own nose, never mind your destiny.'

Jason immediately looked into Ethera's misty blue eyes. Then, kneeling down in front of her, he waved his hand before her face. 'I don't believe it. Sorry, but I never knew...'

He was stopped by the soft touch of the elf girl as she placed a hand on his head.

'Blind I may be,' she said, 'yet I see in other ways.'

Jason stroked her cheek. 'How did Bora do this?'

Tusher butted in and offered an emotive account of the day Ethera was born, and also the last known appearance of the Keeper. He spoke of how, during a difficult labour, her mother had been given one of Bora's herbal concoctions. 'And not only did it kill her,' he went on, 'Ethera were robbed of her eyes.'

However, the elf girl offered her own opinion. 'But others have told me that she were already dying, and that the Keeper saved my life. And who is to say that I wouldn't have been born blind, even without Bora's elixir?'

'I think you're right,' said Jason. 'And I'm sure he was only trying to help.'

Tusher interrupted again. 'Aye, but try telling that to her father. He still holds Bora to blame.'

'And who is your father?' Jason asked Ethera. He then noticed the elves looking uneasily at one another for a moment.

'He be Mans,' said Tusher.

'King of the Dumni,' added Ethera.

Jason grinned. 'Well, that's good news, *Princess*.'

'And why be that?' demanded Tusher.

'Because your king might just be able to tell me why I've been brought into this stupid place.'

'But you be wrong,' Tusher continued, sounding angry. 'Mans will surely slay you if he set eyes upon you. And kill us too for not telling him of our meeting.'

'You mean you haven't told anyone?' asked Jason, his eyebrows raised.

'No,' said Ethera. 'From deep down I had a feeling that we should not, and Tusher agreed as long as he could keep the music box.'

Jason thought for a long moment. 'Okay, he can keep it – just for now.' As he began to walk off, he knew that what he was about to say was really corny – but he couldn't resist it and only just managed to curtail his laughter. 'Take me to your leader.'

A protesting Tusher led the way, with Ethera's hand on his shoulder, followed by Jason closely behind. For a short time they weaved through the woods, undergrowth, and some open stretches of grassland until, from somewhere ahead, the strange wailing noise began once again.

Jason stopped, but the others carried on walking. 'Hold on,' he said. 'What *is* that noise?'

After a few more steps the elves turned to face him.

''Tis evil spirits,' said Tusher, the breeze ruffling his fine hair. 'Best us get out of here.'

'I don't buy it,' said Jason, shaking his head. 'There's no such thing,' before thinking of his current situation and grimacing. 'At least, I didn't *think* there was.'

'Jason is too wise,' said Ethera turning to Tusher. 'He cannot be fooled by a child's plaything.'

The elf boy pondered for a moment, then slowly nodded. 'Follow me…and stay close.'

Soon they were standing at the splayed protruding roots of a massive oak, and Jason cast his eyes upward along its trunk. By now there was an intense mix of rattling and wailing of various pitch, but still he couldn't see anything. 'What on earth is that?' he asked.

'Go see for yourself,' said Tusher. 'And this time, best you do not fall.'

The first thing Jason did before climbing onto the first branch was to check his laces, and once he had given himself the all-clear, he was off.

With each step on the way up, the noises became louder, and within a short time he discovered the cause. Suspended from the middle of the highest branches was a mass of hollowed-out wooden sticks, interspersed with metal rods and chains. They varied in length and thickness, and Jason noticed that as the wind blew harder through the tree, the din increased to the point where it was almost deafening.

Then, just as he was about to make his way back down, he caught some movement in the corner of his eye. Not far away, only this time trotting over the large clearing, was a white horse. On this occasion the animal was being ridden away from the manor house and into the woods on the far side. And sitting atop appeared to be the same long-haired rider who, just for an instant, looked in Jason's direction.

'Just what sort of toy is that?' he asked, his feet once again planted safely on the ground.

'Wind chimes...only lots bigger.' As Ethera said so, a similar sound seemed to arise from other nearby locations. She explained that these devices had been strategically placed on the only exposed boundary of the dell – the side closest to human habitation – and described how their woodland home was protected on its other three sides by precipices so high and terrain so treacherous, that no giant would ever dare to enter.

'But what are these chime things for?' Jason went on.

'The giants be plundering our lands,' said Tusher, 'so us scare them off by making the forest sound haunted. And it works, too.'

Jason shook his head. 'It'll take more than a few wooden sticks and a bit of wind to stop humans coming in here – I know what they're like.' He was then reminded of his most recent contact with his own kind and asked the elves about the girl that he'd seen riding the horse.

The woodlanders faced one another for a moment before turning to Jason.

'She will be one of the giants from yonder abode in the clearing,' said Ethera.

'And they don't dare venture into the dell,' added Tusher.

'That may be,' said Jason, straight-faced. 'But it's only a matter of time before they do.'

Just then he felt something tighten around his ankle, digging painfully into his skin. And before Jason realised what was happening, he was looking up to his feet – and to the treetops. There he swayed to and fro, his hood and backpack skimming the top of the long grass and, as much as he wriggled and struggled and jerked, there seemed to be no escape.

'Well, don't just stand there,' he shouted to the elves, his face quickly reddening. Jason had sent himself into a slow spin, but he was still able to notice the look of shock in their faces. 'Get me down from here.' He continued to revolve at the rope's end and was beginning to feel sick when, from the undergrowth, he heard rustling.

The two elves immediately looked towards the thick vegetation, and Tusher cried: 'No. Leave him alone...he be our friend.'

Jason sensed the panic in the elf boy's voice and, while still in a twirl, scanned around as best he could with his dizzy head. He saw nothing untoward, but why was Tusher so afraid? Until then, he had always seemed to be so much in control.

His question was answered sooner than he could ever have wished. From behind that tree, and that bush, and those brambles; in fact it seemed from everywhere, the creatures emerged. These were taller and broader than the elves he'd already met, and some wore thick leather belts with metal buckles. And they may have had pointed ears, but there the similarities ended.

Jason felt powerless as he watched his little friends being dragged off, kicking and screaming, into the shadows, and the beings that were left behind all focused on him; at least ten of them, he counted.

'Er, hi...I was just passing through and...' Jason wanted to continue speaking, but the air became trapped in his tight chest and his heart began to pound as the group of little people approached ever closer. Something told him that these characters had no desire to listen. Perhaps it was their unsmiling painted black and green faces, the spears and clubs they held aloft, or simply their utter muteness.

His mind was soon drawn to a rabble of fluttering from high above. Through the sweat and tears he saw what looked like vultures circling high above, as if waiting for their next feast. Then the heavy blow arrived, and daylight was no more.

By the time he came round, and with a splitting headache, Jason's face was still just above the ground; only now, he was no longer in a vertical position. The taut netting dug deeply into his cheeks, making his breathing difficult, and he was in no condition to say anything – even if he had wanted to. Then alerting himself more and more, he began to pick up some of the conversation.

'Get on, Div. Thought you was going to knock his block off.'

'Aye, Short. And did you see the look on his ugly face?'

Using every bit of available energy in his body, Jason managed to turn his head to the side. Not only could he now fill his lungs with much needed air, he could also see that the netting was suspended from a long sturdy branch, either side of which a couple of the creatures were providing support with their shoulders. And as he continued to swing from side to side, he caught a better view of the two men leading the group. They walked only a short distance ahead, and he was sure that these were the ones who'd had the brief conversation.

'The giant stirs again,' one of the carriers then shouted.

The group came to an abrupt halt, and the leading two came back to inspect their catch. By then, Jason had snapped his eyes closed and played dead. He held his breath and his heart rattled along, as the elves stuck their spears through to give him a painful prod or two in the ribs.

'*Na!* He be out for the rest of this day, but if he do awaken, you can give him the next clobber, Short.'

Then some wicked laughter. ''Twould be a pleasure. But I'd much rather wait for the stoning.'

As they once again began to wind through the woodland, Jason's stomach began to churn, and he wanted to kick and scream. But he knew that if he did there would be another clubbing in store for him – and that was something he would prefer not to have. And so, as he dangled over the rough track, Jason began to wonder just what his fate *would* be. What did they mean by stoning? Was it what he thought?

Morbid, intrusive thoughts filled his mind for some time, before he dared open his sticky eyes once again to the chattering that had begun to escalate around him. He saw children – elf children – younger looking than Tusher and Ethera. And no longer did he feel like a condemned animal on a slaughterhouse hook; he was now some sort of freak in a travelling circus – something to be mocked.

Through the pain he could smell burning wood and saw that he was now within some sort of settlement. He noticed several small stone buildings – all graced with thatch – outside of which were stacked reed baskets. And groups of tribespeople, standing and gazing in silence at the passing parade; some with barefooted children clutching onto their legs, others holding babies in their arms. Goats and chickens, too, seemed to display a detached fascination with his capture.

Then the chanting commenced, repeating the same words over and over. *'Death to the giant...death to the giant...death to the giant...'* And Jason now did his best to avoid the blows from the rotten fruit and vegetables that began to rain in from all angles.

Soon the procession came to an abrupt halt, and he was dumped onto the sun-baked dusty ground. Crunching against the rock-hard surface was painful, but at least his limbs had more freedom.

As the surrounding netting was being pulled clear, it was time for him to think. Fight or flight...what was it to be? Okay, he was in pain, but he had his trainers on and should still be faster than these guys. Then again, where would he run to? This was their territory – not his own. Bad plan, Jaz. Bad plan. So, could he take them on? There were too many elves to count, and coupled with the number of clubs and spears on show, this idea was also quickly dropped. He was left with only one option.

'My name's Jason, and I mean you no harm,' he managed to mumble. 'Ask Tusher and Ethera.' Staggering to his feet and nursing his aching arms, he waited for a change of facial expression in his audience. It failed to arrive, and the only look they delivered was one of contempt.

'You may fool the young ones with your sorcery.' Div held the mp3 player aloft in one hand, displaying it to the hushed crowd. 'But not me.' He gestured to some of his men who cautiously began to approach Jason, each with a length of rope in his hand.

Short then went to Div and, standing on tiptoes, spoke quietly into his ear. 'Best us wait for the king, don't you think?'

Div shook his head. '*Na*...he be too busy at that blooming circle again.' He placed a hand on his companion's shoulder. 'And when he do return, us'll be honoured as the one's that did slay the giant.'

'But if us kill this beast, will not others come to...'

'*Enough*.' Div's voice echoed around the village. 'You'll do as I say.'

As the menacing band closed in, Jason reckoned that they would reach only about chest height next to him. However, he wasn't up for the fight, and was certain that, as hopeless as the situation seemed, there *would* be a way out. There simply *had* to be. That's what happened in fantasy tales, wasn't it?

'Us can do this the easy way...or t'other,' Div also moved closer.

Jason noticed that this figure, in a brown tunic, was different from the others in their greys and greens. The cuffs at the end of the elf's sleeves were embroidered with scrolling gold patterns, and he carried a small sword on his leather belt. He also had a large wart on the end of his nose.

Soon being bound to the trunk of a nearby oak, Jason offered no resistance. Then the drum roll commenced, and he waited for the inevitable.

Everything began to pass in slow motion once again. That included the first apple-sized missile that was cast when the drumming had ended. It landed with a dull thud next to his foot, rekindling those same very early childhood memories, asking him to leave this place, and to be carried to somewhere else, some other plane...

Then, with Jason's heavy eyelids barely clinging on to consciousness, all activity in the village came to a sudden halt.

'*Stop*, I say.'

The voice had been loud and commanding, and with the remaining dregs of his will to survive, Jason lifted his head to see that everyone had fallen upon one knee with head bowed. And looking to the woods on the left, he saw two men approaching, both with pig-tailed grey hair, one of whom wore a bright red robe.

'What in Arawn's name is this?' Now standing only a stone's-throw away, the man in red looked to Jason, and then to Div. 'I demand an explanation, General.'

The soldier kept his head low. 'Well...you see, Sire. It be like this. Us was...I mean, Short were...'

'*Enough*, you blithering idiot. Now, release the giant.'

'But Sire, he...'

'Just do as I say, man, or I swear you shall be next for a stoning.'

Div immediately gestured to Short, who proceeded to cut the binding away from the teenager's body.

Now free and kneeling, Jason filled his chest with huge gulps of air and turned to the figure that had spoken with such authority. His beard hung long and grey, and he wore a large cross next to his chest; its bright stones matching the colour of his robe.

The man then ordered the people to be upstanding and began to walk over to Jason. However, he was halted for a moment by the excited screams of two elves running towards him – a boy and a girl – holding hands.

'*Father*,' shouted Ethera, just before crashing into the man's leg.

The king placed his hands on the blonde heads of Tusher and Ethera, and then looked to the muttering crowd. 'This giant is welcome in the dell and shall come to no harm here. Now, go back to your homes, and to the woods, and to the plots.' Then turning to Div and Short. 'And you two idiots, I shall have words with later this day. Now, *begone*.'

His companion, Lus, joined the king, and along with the children they went to help Jason to his feet.

'I am Mans, and I bid you welcome.' said the king, his arm offering some support. 'I also beg forgiveness for the way my people did treat you.'

The teenager sensed Ethera sliding her hand into his, and almost immediately he felt relaxed and pain-free. 'My name's Jason, and I was hoping you could tell me why I'm here.'

''Twill become clear when we visit the Great Circle,' said Mans. 'But first you must rest.'

Jason did wonder how they could possibly go from Cockington to Stonehenge without transport, but he was too exhausted to debate the issue.

Mans's cottage was grander than those that Jason had already seen. He was told that it was made of cob and thatch, just like the others, but this one consisted of two levels. And even though the doorway was smaller than he was used to, he had no need to stoop on his way in.

At Jason's request, Ethera and Tusher were allowed to remain with him and the elders as they sat around a large wooden table, where they began to discuss the preceding events.

'I give you my word that never again shall you face such torment at the hands of my people,' said the king after listening to Jason's tale of woe. 'Our dell is your dell.'

The teenager was then encouraged to rest for a while, during which time Ethera attended to his visible cuts and bruises, dabbing them gently with a cloth and cold water.

And so later, following a meal of vegetable broth, it was a refreshed Jason who prepared to leave with the king.

'Father, please can I come with you?' Ethera was clutching his sleeve. 'And Tusher, too?'

Man's shook his head. 'Alas, you cannot, my dear. Stay here with Lus…there are things to be revealed at the Great Circle not for the ears of children.'

Jason saw the look of annoyance and disappointment in their faces, but he didn't feel that it was his place to challenge the king's decision.

Soon walking through the village, Jason noticed how some of the people now offered him a nervous smile, and how others even bowed cautiously before him. It was then up a hillock, down the other side, along a snaking riverbank, through yet more woodland, until eventually they came to a clearing.

'Behold,' said Mans, opening out his arms. 'The Great Circle.'

Dad was wrong; there *were* ceremonial stones in Cockington, after all. However, they appeared nothing like those that he'd seen on the news report from Stonehenge; this large circle consisted of what looked like countless individual rugged black headstones, at the centre of which a massive column of grey projected from the turf.

Jason was told that these outer stones marked the tombs of the tribal ancestors, and that some were thought to be as old as the earth itself. He then asked about the imposing monument at the centre.

''Tis the Stone of Celest; that which foretells our destiny…and yours.'

Moving next to the monolith, Jason narrowed his eyes and ran his fingers over the inscriptions. He encountered a variety of animal figures and decorative swirling patterns. 'What do these mean?' he asked.

The king described how only the elders and monarch have ever had the knowledge to interpret the monolith's runes, before moving his hand over the stone's resident pale green lichens. 'They speak of a boy giant, his eyes as dark as sloes and born to this world on Belenos, who shall arrive before this season's feast. And on that very day, either he shall save the Dumni from his own kind…or condemn us and himself to oblivion.'

Jason grimaced for a moment, then spoke nervously. 'You're having a laugh, aren't you?' He looked to the stone and shook his head. 'I can't walk two steps in this place without something going wrong.'

'Even so, 'tis written.' Mans pointed back to a small, carved section on the stone. 'And bear in mind the dire consequences for you and the tribe should you fail.'

Jason pondered for a while and his tone changed to something more serious. 'The Keeper told me you were the last of the Dumni. Is that right?'

'Aye, there are remnants of other ancient peoples to be found on the Great Moor, but we are the few remaining in these parts.' Mans invited Jason to sit on the grass and told him how great swathes of the Dumni's ancient woodland had been turned by the humans into open fields for their beasts.

'But can't you just talk to them and agree some sort of deal?' Jason suggested.

Mans shook his head. 'For many years we have been in retreat from their destructive ways. And, by the way they treat each other and other living beings, they cannot be trusted.'

'But do they even know you're here?'

'I do not believe so. When it seems they are about to ravage our land, we take what we can, destroy what we cannot, and leave nothing behind but ruins.' Mans then looked Jason in the eye and sounded like someone on the brink of surrender. 'But alas, now there is nowhere left to go.'

Jason turned to the central column and grimaced. 'And does it say *how* I should go about things?'

Mans shook his head and said nothing.

The teenager then stood up and placed his hands on its cool surface. 'I take it you celebrate Belenos around these stones.' He went on to tell the king about what he'd learned from Tusher and Ethera, and about the midsummer celebrations at Stonehenge.

'You mean that in your world the giants do worship the Sun God?' Mans looked astonished.

'Only some do. And where I come from there's going to be a blood moon, as well.'

There was a gasp from the king who rose immediately to his feet. 'Even *I* am not privy to that knowledge. 'Tis only for the Keeper to know when that event shall occur.'

'Well,' said Jason, almost apologetically, 'maybe it's just in my world it's going to happen.'

'You are wrong, my young friend.' A croaky voice interrupted the conversation, and as Jason turned around he saw a familiar figure emerging from the outer circle.

'*Bora*,' said Mans, sounding displeased. 'I should have known you'd be skulking around.'

The Keeper ambled over to join them next to the Stone of Celest. 'Jason speaks the truth,' he said. 'A blood moon *shall* fall on Belenos, even for us here in the dell.'

'But it can't...' Mans then appeared stuck for words.

Bora nodded. 'Aye, 'tis true. On that night we shall surely dance under the red moonlight and pay homage to our new queen.'

Jason was beginning to feel totally lost. 'Look, guys. Can someone tell me what's going on?'

The king looked pale and apparently still struggled to find his tongue.

He was helped by Bora. 'On the said night the ancients shall awaken, and Ethera shall become Queen of the Dumni.'

'*What?*' demanded Jason.

The Keeper attempted to clarify things further. 'With the union of Belenos and the blood moon we enter a time of great change. And it is then that the Dumni shall have their new leader.'

Mans eventually managed to find his words. 'But Ethera yet is a child and in no way ready for such burden.'

Bora looked to the king. 'And two hundred years ago, were you not just a boy when I placed the Moon Cross around your own slender neck?'

Mans appeared to consider the Keeper's words for a moment. 'Aye, but I was without affliction. How shall Ethera lead the tribe in these fearful times when she cannot even lead herself?'

With a frown on his face Jason looked to Bora and interrupted. 'Hold on...did you say that Mans became king two hundred years ago?'

'Your ears did not deceive you, my friend,' said the Keeper. 'The Dumni is a long-lived tribe, and you must understand that Ethera and Tusher are about seventy years old.'

Jason was left standing with his mouth open, allowing the king to return to his own point.

'So answer me, magician of sorts,' he said. 'How shall my dear daughter lead the people?'

Bora smiled. 'That maid sees more than most and possesses gifts not of this world.'

'You can say that again,' said Jason, who went on to explain to Mans what had happened following his fall from the tree.

'I know of her caring touch,' said the king, 'but that what you say is truly wondrous.' Mans still looked bewildered as he turned back to the Keeper. 'From where did these powers arise?'

'From the time of her birth,' said Bora. 'Her eyes and your dear wife were already lost by the time I appeared, and the only thing I could do to help our future queen was to bestow a blessing upon her.'

'And what was that?' demanded Mans, still sounding unconvinced.

'We have just heard of her healing power,' said Bora. 'But she has also gained the ears of an owl and the nose of a fox. All these things together shall serve her better than any eyes could ever do.'

Jason deduced from the blank expression on the king's face that he was having difficulty in grasping all that he was hearing. He then placed his hand on Mans's shoulder. 'From what I've heard her say and see her do, I think Ethera will make a great queen.'

'And it must come to pass,' added Bora. 'The ways of old cannot be changed.'

The king slowly nodded in apparent resignation. 'When we return to the village I shall give Ethera the news of her accession...and of the true nature of our plight.'

As Mans and Jason began the return journey, the Keeper disappeared behind the central stone.

On their arrival at the king's cottage, Jason noticed that Mans gave his daughter a longer embrace than he had done earlier that day, and he detected a tear in his eye.

The king then looked to Lus. 'Please, stay a while. I have news for you and my daughter.'

'I want Tusher to be here, too,' demanded Ethera.

'Please, father. Can I?' Tusher's eyes were pleading as he turned to Lus, who eventually gave a single nod of approval.

For some time Mans did most of the talking around the table, describing in detail the critical position of the tribe, the predicted arrival of Jason, and finally the blood moon with its own consequences. The king then held his daughter's hand. 'So your time has come, Ethera. And I shall be here to help you.'

She nodded and smiled in return, but remained silent.

Mans now looked to Jason. 'I must tell the folk – one and all – of your purpose here. Yet we know nothing of your intentions.'

Jason had already been considering what his next move should be. And remembering the words of advice from the Keeper, he had reached his decision. 'Even after seeing and hearing what I have today, I still know next to nothing about your people. And so, with your permission, I'd like to spend more time with you here in the village and out there in the dell. Only then can I begin to think about how to help.'

A smile came to Ethera's face. 'If you like you can come with Tusher and me into the forest tomorrow. There is much more for you to learn in there; things you never could imagine.'

'Cool…that's what I was thinking,' said Jason. 'Just make sure you get my music box back from that Div bloke.' He then started grinning. 'And, if there's time, I'll show you and Tusher a few more moves.'

Mans rose to his feet and brought the meeting to an end. 'So be it. Ethera and Tusher shall pass the morrow with Jason, while I prepare the people for what lies ahead…whatever that may be.'

Chapter Six

If the word of Mans had any value, Jason would now have little to fear in this leafy world. And with this in mind the next morning he felt more at ease following his friends through the winding paths.

Along the way they veered off the main track, and Jason soon found himself sitting by the side of a gurgling brook. The tangles of nearby brambles hosted a collection of blackberries, none of which was ripe for eating. However, he'd already noticed his little companions foraging around at ground level and decided to investigate. At first sight he couldn't see what they were looking for, before Tusher produced a small red berry in the palm of his hand.

'Try it.' The elf boy offered what looked like a tiny strawberry.

Jason accepted the invitation and held it by the stalk. And after chancing a dainty nibble, he was soon nodding in approval. 'Mmm…they ain't as sweet as this where I come from.' He was then quickly down on his hands and knees, delving into the mass of spreading plants, where he began to gorge himself with more of the succulent fruit.

After satisfying his hunger, Jason quenched his thirst with the clear water from the stream. No cup was required this time – just a smooth sucking action from his lips as he lay on his belly and held his face over the glistening surface. Then, resting back on the bank with the high sun warming his face, he saw that the elves had begun to fill their small satchels with the leaves from the strawberry plant.

'Don't tell me you can eat those as well,' he said to them.

Ethera nodded. 'Good for belly and bones.' She then pointed to the arching bramble vines. 'And those scaldhead leaves are used for skin maladies.'

And for some time afterwards, as he strolled with the elves through the wooded valley, Jason gained a fair insight into the nutritional and medicinal properties of countless leaves, roots, berries, and fungi. He learned of treatments and cures for bleeding, pain, depression, skin problems, and a host of other disorders, and the interactive experience at the hands of his young teachers proved to be a good deal more exciting than any science lesson he'd ever endured at school. He thanked them for their patient explanation for the details that he found difficult to grasp, but ended with something that had been on his mind since arriving in the dell.

'Does anyone eat meat here?' Jason noticed the elves turning to one another with a look on their faces that may have suggested offence. 'You know…animals,' he went on, grimacing.

'We would only kill to prevent suffering or to save our own lives,' said Ethera. 'There are tales of our ancestors hunting wild beasts for food, but we have long since learned to live without flesh.'

For a moment Jason thought of his favourite beefburger and felt a little uneasy. 'So, er...why's that?'

'Why should any sentient being be slaughtered to satisfy our hunger?' said Tusher, a stern look on his face. 'Animals need us, and us them.'

But Jason shook his head. 'Surely they're here for the benefit of humans – and the Dumni, I suppose. After all, we're superior to all other living things, aren't we?'

Ethera sighed. 'I see you have much yet to learn.'

'And how's that, then?'

Before the conversation advanced any further, the three of them had sat upon a fallen oak at the side of the trail.

'Consider the great tysca.' Ethera tilted her head back, as if looking beyond the towering treetops.

Jason followed her movements. Initially, he saw nothing in the sky other than a few fluffy clouds, but then from behind the crown of a silver birch there appeared some activity. A dark shape had emerged, which circled ever higher – seemingly without much effort – and was soon gliding menacingly over their position.

'Do you have his keen eye, or claws, or speed, or grace?' Ethera went on. 'I think not...so in what sense are you better than he?'

Jason had never heard of such a bird, but he reckoned that she was talking about a buzzard. 'All right, in some ways maybe we're not superior, but isn't the tysca killing and eating other animals?'

Tusher nodded. 'Aye, but it be the only way for him to survive. And as you have witnessed this very day, the forest provides all that us need.' At that moment a solitary wasp buzzed over to Tusher and settled on the back of his hand.

'And what about them?' Jason asked, pointing a shaky finger to the stinging insect. 'Surely, they're just a pest and serve no purpose.'

Ethera laughed. 'Equally, the vespa may deem you to be a pest. And his purpose is to *be* – just like you.'

'But what good is your vespa to anyone?'

Tusher gently blew the wasp into the breeze. 'He feasts on the flowers and helps to make their fruits.' Then looking directly at Jason. 'And what about you? What good do you serve? For, from what be said, the humans bring nothing but destruction.'

'Boys, boys, boys,' said Ethera, interrupting the increasingly heated debate. 'All life has equal value – and beauty and purpose, too. And that includes Dumni and humans.'

'But you've got animals,' Jason went on. 'I saw them for myself.'

'Aye,' Ethera agreed, 'but even a human must know that animals can provide sustenance in other ways.'

Jason recalled the cheese that he'd eaten at the Keeper's cottage, yet he still persisted. 'Well, some of you wear animal skins…I saw them in the village.'

'That is true,' the elf girl added, 'but only from those beasts that die in nature's way.'

Following a sigh, Jason slowly nodded his head. 'This is the sort of stuff my dad talks about. He doesn't eat meat either, and there's lots of others just like him.'

'Well, maybe the Dumni and giants be closer than us believe.' Tusher then slid down from the tree trunk, and after doing so a grin appeared on his face. 'Did you get your music box back?'

'Yeah, and I remember saying I'd show you a thing or two.' Jason stood up and opened his backpack to retrieve the mp3 player, but the first thing that came to hand was his mobile phone.

'What manner of finding be that?' Tusher pointed to the slim device before Jason had the chance to replace it.

'Oh, it's just something that we humans use to talk to each other when we're far apart.'

Tusher frowned. 'Show us, then.'

Jason returned the phone to his bag. 'Sorry, but it'll only work in my own world. Anyway, if you guys live as long as I've been told, you might have your own one day.'

'At least try.' The elf boy sounded ever more impatient.

Jason shook his head. 'There's no point. Just trust me when I say it won't work here.'

Tusher grunted, before a grinning Ethera joined in. 'The Dumni can send messages, too,' she said.

'Really?' Jason smiled wryly, slinging his bag over his shoulder. 'And how's that?'

Tusher promptly perched himself once more onto the log, before cupping his hands closely over his mouth. 'Just you listen to this,' he said, sounding cocky.

With subtle finger and cheek movements the elf went on to perform an enchanting array of musical whistles, interspersed with penetrating trills and chatters. He repeated a few of the chords over and over, and by the time he had finished, it seemed that most of the feathered beings within the forest had joined in.

Jason waited for the melody to abate, then looked to the elf. 'That was *brill*. What bird was it?'

''Twere Mavis.' Tusher went on to describe a smallish brown bird with a spotted breast.

To Jason it sounded like a song thrush. 'So what does it mean when you sing that one?'

''Tis just a simple greeting to let our friends know where we are,' said Ethera. 'And some of the music you did hear in return came from Dumni in other parts of the dell.'

'*Cool*. And can you do more?'

Tusher duly obliged with some impressive imitations of a wide range of birds, each time explaining what the song represented. He ended with a cooing wood pigeon, before saying: 'And with that one I've just told some of the others where they lovely berries be.'

'So how do they know it's you and not a real bird?' Jason asked.

''Tis easy once you learn how,' said Tusher. 'Them all might sound the same to you, but us can even tell which *one* of our friends be calling. Every song be just a bit different to the rest.'

At that moment Ethera smiled towards her companion; cheekily, thought Jason.

'Go on, Tusher,' she said. 'Give it your best go.'

The elf boy hesitated for a moment. 'Be that a good idea?'

'Aye,' replied Ethera, sounding enthusiastic. 'Please, Tusher. Do it…just for me…*please.*'

'Oh, alright, lass. Just for you,' came the sighed response.

There followed a piercing and sustained high-pitched cackle, so loud that Jason was forced to place his hands over his ears. And only when Tusher had finished his piece did he dare lower them.

'What on earth was that?' Jason still had a pained expression on his face.

''Tis Blackie when he be in trouble,' said Tusher. 'And it be a call to other Dumni when us need help.'

Jason suspected that the elf was talking about a blackbird, and after a quick glance around he sniggered. 'Are you sure it works, because no one has come to save you from the big bad giant?'

Tusher lay back onto the log, looking relaxed. 'Just you have a *proper* look, and then tell me so.'

This time Jason gave the long grass and clumps of dock plants some closer attention, but still he could see nothing. Then, lifting his eyes to the fluttering sounds within the trees, he searched the creaking boughs, before turning to Tusher once again. 'Sorry, mate. Looks like your friends have deserted you.'

Tusher had a little laugh to himself and sat upright. 'You can come out now, lads. 'Tis only me showing our giant a trick or two.'

Jason wheeled around to inspect the crackling that had begun in the nearby undergrowth. As the grass parted, he counted eight young elves – boys and girls – standing only just a few paces away, all of them bare footed with blonde hair, and each with a stone in their hands. Then his eyes turned to the tuneful whistling from deep within the tree crowns, which was quickly followed by numerous small figures clambering like green-clad monkeys down the trunks to the forest floor. Every tree yielded a handful of the creatures, and a short moment later there were simply too many to number.

The growing band of woodland dwellers now included a few older individuals that Jason remembered from his initial capture, and some carried bows, arrows, and spears. His heart began to race, and he backed off towards his two friends.

''Tis all right, Jason,' said Ethera, squeezing his hand. 'They won't bother you now.'

'Aye,' added Tusher, before addressing his fellow Dumni. 'I thank you for your presence but, as you can see, us be just larking.'

'As long as you be sure,' shouted a member of the clan, one with blackened teeth and matted hair.

He and all the others then merged seamlessly into the surrounding flora, leaving nothing behind but a few levelled trails in their wake.

In the near quiet that ensued, Jason turned to Tusher. 'Now *that* was really something. But why didn't you do the call when you first saw me?'

'We thought we should just hide,' said Ethera.

'...but never reckoned on you climbing the same blooming tree,' added Tusher.

'Even when you did,' Ethera went on, 'we never did believe you'd go so high that you'd find us perched where we were. And Tusher never did the call because the din would've given us away.'

'And when you did fall,' said Tusher, 'there were no need for help...us thought you was dead.'

'Well, I'm just glad you didn't,' said Jason, 'otherwise I would've been a goner.' Then opening his backpack, a smile appeared on his face as he produced the mp3 player. 'Come on. Let's get breakin', *man*.'

However, before Jason even had the chance to switch it on, Ethera had placed her hands either side of her head. Her eyes were closed, as though in deep concentration.

'Husht...the two of you,' she quietly ordered. 'I hear a nag on the trail, and it's a-coming this way.'

Jason shut his own eyes and listened as deeply as he could into the surrounding forest. But other than the occasional twitter from the bird life, the rustling of leaves in the breeze, and the distant music from the wind chimes, he detected nothing. 'Are you sure?' he whispered to Ethera.

'She can hear the moon rise,' said Tusher. 'And if there be a nag, there be a giant, too.' He then pointed to a nearby thicket, which stood at the side of a long ditch. ''Tis best us hide yonder.'

Jason led the way as they waded through the grass, with Tusher and Ethera clutching hands just a step behind. And once safely within the shadows, they sat and waited, and watched, and listened.

For a long moment Jason was aware only of the now familiar sounds of the forest. But then, very gradually, he did hear something that was a bit like hooves beating upon hardened earth, and he rose to his feet. He attempted to peer through the shrubs towards the dirt track, but the leathery foliage of a rhododendron obscured his view. Then, moving forward a little to move the leaves to one side, Jason trod upon an old branch and produced a snapping sound so loud that it seemed to ricochet from tree to tree throughout the wood.

'You daft galoot,' said Tusher quietly, grabbing Jason's wrist. 'You'll have us all killed.'

'*Sorry.*' Jason winced – and not only through what he had just done. His wrist ached with the surprising strength of the elf's grip.

The muffled clumping moved ever closer as Jason stood motionless under the arching branches of the shrub. He could feel his heart thumping at his chest as, either side of him, his Dumni friends froze like statuesque goblins.

Jason then caught a flash of white through the shimmering greenery, before witnessing a large animal emerge into an opening on the track. Upon its back sat a girl having a good all-round look, ducking every now and again to avoid the lower branches. And as the visitors came to a rest next to the old trunk where Jason had sat with the others only a short time before, he was pretty sure that this was the same horse and rider he'd spotted when climbing the trees. Then, just for a moment, the breeze picked up, and the animal became increasingly restless, wildly nodding and whinnying loudly.

'Hush now, George. It's only the wind blowing through the trees.' The girl moved a hand to gently stroke the horse's mane, and leaning forward she whispered a few words in his ear.

Very soon the beast was at ease, and the rider dismounted, before she tethered the reins loosely around an overhanging branch. Her wavy locks flowed freely from under a soft flat hat, the green velvet of which glistened in strands of sunlight. The headwear matched her jacket and long dress, which was puffed at the bottom, and as she stood with whip in white-gloved hand, she narrowed her eyes and peered along the ditch at the rhododendron, next to which frolicked two young rabbits.

For a brief moment Jason held his breath, sure that he and his friends would be spotted. His pulse was still racing as he crouched ever lower into the cover of the shrub, where he joined the others in a hunched posture. And only when she turned her attention elsewhere, was he able to vent a silent sigh of relief into his sleeve.

However, it seemed like this inquisitive visitor to the forest had no wish to leave in a hurry. She had already removed her hat and gloves, carefully placing them onto the rough grass, and stayed around the same spot for quite some time – sniffing and picking at the plants on the side of the track. Eventually, with her hands brimming with wild flowers, she returned to the horse and placed them into a pouch on the large leather saddle. After doing so, she turned around and scanned left to right.

'I know that you are in here somewhere…so you may as well come out.' Her young voice sounded clear and confident. 'Come now. I heard you chattering as I came along the track…as did George, whose hearing is far beyond my own.'

Jason turned to his companions. Tusher frowned and shook his head, before Ethera, with hands over her face, offered her opinion.

'I feel a goodness in that there maid,' she said quietly.

Tusher grabbed her sleeve. 'Be you mad, lass? Do you wish this dell swarming with even more giants? I says us stay here until she be gone.'

Jason intervened, placing his hand gently upon the elf boy's shoulder, then spoke in a quiet but firm manner. 'Tush, mate. Whether you like it or not, *nothing* is going to stop humans coming in here. And unless you begin to reach out to them, your dell, and the Dumni, will be lost...*forever.*'

'But us can't trust them.' Even within the dark shade, the elf's scowl was evident.

'Well,' said Jason, 'let's look at your other options. You could stand your ground, fight...and be slaughtered. Or you can continue to run – but where would you go?'

Tusher grunted, but after a short moment he slowly nodded his head.

'So be it.' Ethera now sounded decisive. 'You may go to the maid, but speak nothing of us until we know for sure what her intentions may be.'

Jason squinted through the greenery to the girl who was still looking around the woods. And after a final nod of approval from the elves, he parted the leaves and stood in the open, just a short distance from the horse and rider.

'Ah...there you are, my mysterious friend.' The girl lifted the hem of her dress and moved a couple of steps towards Jason, who was rooted to the spot. 'You may be trespassing on my father's land, but I do not bite...I promise.' She smiled and beckoned him over with her hand.

Jason jumped down into the shallow ditch, trying especially hard to appear as composed as possible, and he moved slowly through the rough grass, pausing just a few paces short of the track. Now closer, he noticed the sparkling golden embroidery within the dress, along with its frilly white cuffs and the shiny metal studs on the jacket. For a long moment he gaped and remained motionless, attempting to come to terms with her strange but elegant style of clothing. It was as if the whole scene – the girl included – had been plucked from a museum and assembled in front of him.

'Are you going to stand and gawk all day?' she asked. 'Or will you at least have the decency to tell me your name?'

Jason had a problem finding his words, and also with removing his gaze from the girl's unblemished face. He couldn't help but become entranced by her striking green eyes, and he began to experience a tingling sensation throughout his entire body. There was also a feeling of excitement; a strange all-over high that he'd never before encountered, and just to compound matters, his legs developed a slight wobble.

'I say. Is catching flies a pastime of yours?'

Only then did Jason realise that he was standing with his mouth wide. 'Er, sorry. I was...er...I was just looking at...'

'...my dress?'

'Yeah, that's it...your dress...its really nice.' Jason felt his bodily functions return to something approaching normal, but he still sensed a pleasant inward rush as he walked closer.

'I'm Jason.' He thought it best not to offer a grubby handshake.

The girl smiled. 'Megan's my name...and your clothes are nice, too.' She then held a delicate pale hand over her mouth to help suppress a quiet giggle.

Jason looked at his twenty-first century clothing. 'Oh, yeah...well, that's Exeter for you.' And how he managed to keep a straight face, Jason didn't know.

Megan soon managed to control herself. 'So what is a young man all the way from that fair diocese doing in the bushes? And who were you talking to?' She sounded inquisitive, rather than belligerent.

Jason now knew that he would have to choose his words carefully. 'I'm here with my dad for a few days, and we went in there to look at a blackbird's nest.'

'Really?' The girl looked around. 'So where is he now?'

Jason hesitated for a moment, then said: 'Oh...he flew away.'

The girl laughed. 'I meant your father, *Silly*.'

'Yeah, right. Er, he's away back to the old cottage...the one at the far side of the forest.' This was the first thing that had come to mind, and Jason tried not to grimace.

Megan appeared to consider his answer for a moment, then frowned. 'I do not know of any such place.'

Jason produced a nervous cough, before saying: 'Well...er...it's well hidden by the trees and really hard to see.' He then quickly changed the subject. 'Anyway, you said your father owns this wood. Who is he exactly?'

The girl didn't seem to notice his ploy and smiled once again. 'His real name is Stephen, but no one's allowed to call him that.' For a short time Megan went on to explain how, on the death of her grandfather six years before, her own father had inherited the vast estate to become the tenth Earl of Cockington. Beginning with the manor house and the immediate surrounding area, Jason was told that the grounds stretched for around two miles through the forest to the coast, and for about five miles inland.

'Wow,' said Jason. 'But he wouldn't *really* mind me in here, would he?'

'I'm afraid so, but he never comes into this part of the estate...he's very superstitious.' Megan sat on the fallen tree trunk, where she told of her father's belief that the woods were haunted, and how even his own daughter was forbidden to enter the combe.

'But you're in here now,' said Jason.

'Yes, but that's because I don't believe in ghosts or goblins...that's all nonsense.'

'So what about the creepy sounds around here?' asked Jason. 'Are you not afraid of them?'

Megan laughed. 'Why should I fear a few noisy sticks hanging in the trees?'

'So you've seen them, too?' Jason was surprised by her response.

'Of course, I have…a few times.' Megan glanced around the treetops. 'Somehow I feel attracted to this place, but I cannot tell my father, you must understand.' She then stood up. 'Anyway, time moves on, and I'd better return home before he worries.' With that, the girl began to twirl a lock of her hair and looked shyly to Jason. 'Would you like to walk with me to the clearing?'

For Jason the request was nothing short of rhetorical. It wasn't an every day event for him to be invited for a stroll through an enchanted forest with a total stranger – and a pretty one at that. But before he could answer, he was struck by that same head-to-toe tingling sensation and once again felt his face burn. 'Er…well…'

'Oh, come now…it shall not take long, and on the way you can tell me why you were climbing that great oak yesterday.' Megan explained how, when she had seen someone in the tree, she had decided to investigate. Only, when she arrived, there was no sign of anyone.

'That could've been dangerous,' said Jason, knowing that if Megan had been there just a little sooner, she could have faced a stoning as well. 'You might have got lost or something.'

By the time Megan went to remount, she had once more donned her full regalia. Then climbing into the saddle, she rested one black boot upon an oversized stirrup, and fed her right leg between two horns atop. And although she had ended up facing forward, both her legs were to one side.

'Are you sure that's right?' asked Jason, frowning.

Megan simply smiled, before asking Jason to lead the way back down the track.

Setting off, he managed a discreet thumbs-up to his little friends in the shrub, and he was just glad that none of his other mates could see him now, even though he knew that they would all be green with envy.

On the short journey he grimaced only a little as he told her all about his fascination with birds, and how he had climbed the tree to have a look inside a crow's nest. He then thought of the bird songs that he'd only just heard from Tusher, most of which were still fresh on his mind, and came up with an idea – although he wouldn't dare try to repeat the elf's masterly performance. Instead, he made do with listening for a particular bird to announce itself, before attempting to impress his new friend with his incredible knowledge.

'That one you heard just now...well, that's a robin marking his territory.'

And by the time the trees opened up into a grassy field, Jason believed that he had correctly identified most of the feathered wildlife within the forest.

'*Well done.*' Megan sounded impressed. 'And not bad for someone from the city.'

Jason did feel a bit guilty, but not too much. 'Are you going home now...I mean...right this minute?' Now he had difficulty looking her in the eye.

Megan sighed. 'I am afraid so. Father can be strict when he wants to.' And after a short awkward silence, she said farewell and trotted off.

Jason sensed the sky turning grey as he watched Megan melt away.

She then glanced back and shouted. 'Perhaps we can meet again tomorrow.'

'Oh, yeah...only if you really want to, that is.' As Jason replied, the sun warmed his face once again.

'Same place, same time,' Megan cried, just before disappearing into a hollow.

A grinning sixteen year-old leapt over the thin wall of bramble vines and back into the forest, where the bird song seemed to ring out louder than ever, as if a feathered choir had been assembled to celebrate his return. He had also developed a spring in his step as he made his way along the track to the spot where he'd first met Megan, and he began to wonder if his little friends would still be there.

The chattering voices from a short way behind soon delivered an answer. Coming to a halt and spinning round, he saw Tusher and Ethera walking hand in hand. And once closer, he noticed that they were both smiling, with the elf boy carrying a red squirrel upon his shoulder.

'Hi, guys,' said Jason. 'I suppose you want to know what happened?'

'Us know what happened, all right.' Tusher went on to say how he and Ethera had never been more than a few paces away and had seen and heard everything – including Megan's assertion that her father owned the lands *and* Jason's attempted birdsong lesson.

Jason sighed and sounded displeased. 'Glad you enjoyed the show…and I suppose you know I'm going to see her again tomorrow?'

'Aye,' said Ethera, 'and I sense something between the two of you.' She ended with a knowing smile on her face.

Jason glowered. 'And what do you mean by that?'

'Oh, get on,' said Tusher, his furry friend now resting on his other shoulder. 'I did see the way your eyes nearly fell out.'

Jason then gave a prolonged shake of his head. 'No…that's where you're wrong, Tush. She's nothing special…and anyway, what would *I* want with a stupid girl?'

'Well, she has a shine for you, my dear boy,' said Ethera. 'And I know how girls are.'

Jason only just maintained his serious face and refused to be drawn any further. 'In case you've forgotten, I'm here to save the Dumni. So less of the silly talk. *Okay?*' Then looking to Tusher. 'And by the way, that squirrel doesn't suit you.'

With time moving on they decided that any further breakdancing tuition could wait until later. Instead, and for quite some time after this, a stick-wielding Tusher led the way at a fair pace through the forest – Ethera having named their next goal as the far end of the valley. They kept mostly to the established trails, but also veered off occasionally to forge routes of their own through dense carpets of wild flowers.

Trudging a couple of steps behind, Jason eventually managed to divert his thoughts and feelings away from Megan, and he was now beginning to truly appreciate the beauty of this unspoiled land. Standing at the top of a waterfall, the crashing din as it cascaded into a dark ravine reminded him of a strong wind rushing through trees, only much louder, and he simply couldn't resist climbing down the slope to have a closer look.

After this, Jason encountered a host of murmuring streams that meandered like restless snakes through arching branches, within which no plastic carrier bag or soft-drink can had yet taken up permanent residence. Stopping at one of them and peeling off his trainers and socks, he couldn't help but rest on the bank for a long moment just to relish the cold water over his clammy bare feet.

Further on he met boulders the size of cars, with thick coats of damp moss. Up he would climb, digging his fingertips into the cool green covering, before sliding down the other side.

Then, coming across a family of leafless oaks, he noticed how they creaked like ancient arthritic corpses; yet even in their state of permanent rest, still reaching out to protect the younger growth around them.

Some time later, after clambering down the winding track of a briar-filled hillside, the forest thinned out and they reached their destination.

Words failed Jason as he stood at the edge of a flat clearance that measured several times the size of the cricket field he had seen in Cockington. It sat nestled within densely wooded slopes, which rose sufficiently high to ensure that anything growing here was favoured with shelter from any strong wind, and he imagined that on the other side of these hills would be the sheer drops that kept the humans at bay. And although the natural landscape seemed to bless the Dumni with security from potential invaders, Jason felt an inner jolt as he suddenly realised that they truly were nothing more than prisoners within their own little world.

He then noticed how the plain had been divided into numerous smaller plots, each of which had at least two of the little people tending to the crops within. 'Amazing,' he said, before turning to Ethera, 'and your people are working hard.'

'They have to,' she replied. 'There are many bellies to fill.' The elf girl went on to describe a whole range of produce that was harvested from this fertile scene, including a variety of vegetables, apples, berries, nuts, honey and cereals. Not only food – from something called flax they were able to produce clothing, and also oil for burning in their lamps. She finished by saying that the grown-ups worked the fields, whereas the younger Dumni remained within the forest to find what they could in there.

Next, Jason heard how this arable land was shared between the different hamlets within the Dumni community, and that the village where the king resided was the largest of these. Also, this wasn't the only cultivated area; there were many smaller plots within the forest. 'So, how many Dumni live in the dell?' he asked, with genuine concern etched into his face.

'Four hundred,' said Tusher. 'Give or take a score or two.'

Together with his friends, Jason spent a short time at the location, grasping the opportunity to sample its offerings. He felt his heart sink – and his shoulders – with the weight of responsibility that was beginning to rest upon them. He had just witnessed two of the workers, a man and a woman, trudge past him as they returned to their homes after a day's toil. He noticed the sweat dripping from their weather-tracked faces and the look of despair in their pale eyes as one of them said: 'Thank you for helping us.'

This was no game and no fun-filled adventure, he now realised. And these beings might have had pointed ears and may only have been half his size, but they were people – just like him.

With deepening thoughts on his mind, Jason made the long trek back to the village. On reaching the smoky and musical clearing, he looked to the centre of the settlement and saw that several large groups had formed around a stack of flaming logs. He felt a lump appear in his throat on hearing that, despite the tribe's present problems, the singing, drinking, and dancing in great circular formations were in preparation for the approaching midsummer festivals.

Jason was then ushered inside Mans's cottage for some welcome hot food, before providing Ethera's father with an update of the day's events. And after he had delivered his account of the meeting with Megan, he watched as the king shook his head in apparent exasperation.

'It comes as no surprise that the father of this maid claims these lands as his own,' said Mans. 'This has been the way of the giants for countless generations.' The king went on to ask Jason if he had yet devised a clear plan with which to save his people.

'As I said to Ethera,' Jason began, 'I think the only way forward is to talk with the humans. So, when I meet up with Megan tomorrow I'll try and find out a bit more about her father, because it seems to me that he's the main man around here…other than you, of course.' With the scowling look on the king's face, he was just glad to have sneaked in those last few words.

Tusher grinned. 'Aye, but just be sure to keep your mind on the job in hand and not on other things.'

Jason narrowed his eyes, and under the table he delivered a sharp rap with the toe of his size eight trainer. 'What's that you're saying, Tush?' He finished with eyebrows raised.

'Nothing…' came the whimpered response, as the elf slid his hand underneath to massage his shin.

Chapter Seven

At dawn the following day Jason was at odds with his fledgling love affair with the marvels of nature. For some time he'd squirmed around on a bed of straw, covering both ears and cursing under his breath. However, the penetrating alarm call of a cockerel had overcome his vain efforts, and being midsummer, daybreak was unfeasibly early. With each intrusive shriek he thought to get up and throttle the stupid thing, but he wasn't able even to find the energy to raise his head from the musty bedding. So there he remained, worn out, screwing his eyes tightly shut, trying but failing to blot out this noisy world.

Even after the din had long since abated, Jason couldn't drift back to sleep, and his mind shifted from feathered strangulation to the task ahead.

To begin with, he had been told by Megan to meet at the same time, but when would that be? Didn't anyone have a watch in this place? Also, assuming she even bothered to turn up, should he just come out with it and tell her that he was from the year two thousand and eight? Was this even crazier than the notion of a tribe of elves fighting for their very existence in her backyard? Jason then remembered her saying that she wasn't superstitious, and he didn't dare to imagine what her response might be.

And what about her father? Jason had heard that he could be strict, yet what did this mean? Could he simply ask Megan for a meeting with her dad and explain everything to him? But hold on, he then thought, attempting to recall some distant history lesson. Wasn't there a chance that they would still believe in witchcraft in these days and burn him at the stake? Or even worse; mightn't he be sent to Australia?

The unanswered questions continued as, eventually, Jason managed to crawl to the shutters of the upstairs room. Swinging them outwards, the glare from the morning sun struck his squinting face.

Looking down with bleary eyes to the central area of the dusty hamlet, the little cottages stood dormant around the smouldering ashes of the previous night's fire. The only visible sign of life was the older man and woman who were collecting eggs from a netted chicken coop. No free-roaming fowl to see; Jason surmising that the birds would have been placed into the pen for the night, well away from the prying eyes of forest predators. He had already encountered the fox, but were wolves around in Torquay at this point in time? Or bears, even? He didn't know, for sure.

Before long, Jason was once more sitting at the table in the main downstairs' chamber and, helping himself to bread and cheese, was soon joined by his friends. He asked them how they managed to keep track of time in the forest and was enthralled by the complex, yet simple, response.

The elves explained how the annual cycle, starting with the winter solstice, comprised of four distinct seasons which, for Jason, was straightforward enough. Then he learned that the year was further divided into thirteen months, with the full moon appearing in the middle of each four-week period. However, he did raise an eyebrow when informed that, for the Dumni, the day would officially begin at sunset. How *strange*.

Although he was also provided with the names of the months and days, Jason thought it better not to attempt to repeat them; they sounded like they had come directly from a Welsh language programme that he'd once seen on telly. Just knowing that most were named after gods or ancestral figures was sufficient.

The conversation ultimately reached the topic of the day itself, where Ethera explained how it was divided into eight distinct periods, all with yet more unpronounceable names – as far as Jason was concerned. Each would be determined by the position of the sun or moon relative to a fixed landmark within the dell; generally, one of the great trees. Other things, too, could assist in time measurement – like animal behaviour, the flowering of shrubs, or the moisture content within tree moss.

As Jason eventually came around to asking the elves about the timing of the meeting with Megan, he had to work hard to conceal his growing excitement, and the questions now entering his mind were more personal in nature. Like, what should he wear? Should he wash his hair...and with what? Would it be time to change his underwear? Or could he squeeze another day out of them? And were his socks and trainers too smelly?

All at once, and for the first occasion that he could remember, these things seemed very important. Fortunately, after hearing that he should meet Megan just as the sun reached its peak, Jason was afforded with the time he needed to attend to such matters.

The early morning dew had burned off before he visited the stream that babbled through the briars at the rear of the king's cottage. Summer it may have been, but the water still felt like ice on his face. And was that a pimple he felt on his maturing chin? He would *have* to attend to that. Then it was time to fix his bed-head. He had asked for shampoo, but in return was handed a bowl of lavender oil.

With the stream so cold, Jason didn't have the courage to duck his head under the water. Instead, he wet his hair with his hands and massaged into it some of the fragrant contents from the bowl. Afterwards, without the use of a mirror, he didn't have a clue how he looked, but at least he smelled nice – *and* had been overcome with an inner calm.

At Mans's insistence the remainder of Jason's morning would be spent acquainting himself with the day to day life of the tribe. And although the inhabitants had been informed of their precarious situation, the king had emphasised the importance of carrying on with life as normal.

Jason quickly established that the elves had much in common with people like himself. Opening a door to one of the buildings, he observed a group of younger children. They sat huddled upon two logs, which had been carved to produce sturdy benches. And as he stooped inside the doorway and peered into the shady room, the youngsters fell silent and turned to stare at him. Some appeared fearful, others curious. He apologised and urged them to carry on with their work. One by one they slowly turned around to face the grown-up at the front of the room and, as he guiltily closed the panelled door to walk away, Jason concluded that this was the village school.

Some of the adults had long since gone to labour in their fields, yet those left behind had no easier job. Going back to the stream, Jason encountered a small mill, together with churning waterwheel. Not far away stood another cottage; its chimney belching grey plumes into a windless sky. He soon established its purpose as his nostrils were filled with the delicious smell of freshly baked bread.

Another aroma that he found pleasing was that which wafted from a building known as the malting house. Not only did it brew a fine ale, he also heard about the production of cyser – an exotic alcoholic blend made from honey and apples.

Following his relaxing lavender experience, this browse around the village soon reminded Jason of the responsibilities that were stacking up. The lives of men, women, and children were now in his hands – and he'd better be up to the task. The time was arriving for him to save the Dumni, and *nothing* would get in his way, he resolved.

A gleaming Jason, equipped with fresh boxer shorts and clean socks, was later advised that it was time to leave. And soon he was standing outside the king's cottage, where he looked to those who had gathered to see him off – news travelled fast in these parts, it seemed.

Just then, several infants grouped around his legs, with some of them clinging like limpets to his jeans. He could see from their playful sunny faces that they didn't perceive things as the grown-ups had done – it was all a big game for them, he reckoned.

One of them, a young girl, passed to him a few tiny figures made with twigs and bound with wool. As Jason held the delicate creations in the palm of his hand, she told him that they were worry dolls. All that he had to do was tell them his problems before going to sleep, place the dolls under his pillow, and all his fears will have disappeared by the morning. Thinking back to the disturbed night that he'd just endured, Jason only wished that she had presented her gift a day earlier. Thanking the youngster, he gently stroked her cheek and placed the collection into his pocket.

Jason then inhaled deeply and turned once more to the others. 'Promise that no one will follow me…I need to do this on my own.'

Nearby, Mans and Ethera nodded. But there was a moment's hesitation from Tusher before he offered his own approval, albeit with a face like thunder. Jason then slung his backpack over his shoulder and recalled the words of advice from his father that he'd heard on the drive to Cockington. *'It's making a difference that matters.'* And with his head held high, he set off.

However, the determination that Jason had felt as he departed was soon wavering, and before long his thoughts could venture no further than a meeting with a girl. One with long blonde hair, a nice smile, and a confidence that he admired. And something else – she didn't even chew gum or wear make-up.

When he eventually arrived at the meeting place, the only apparent life forms were native to the forest. And perching onto the log, Jason was careful not to disturb a nearby clump of honey fungus. Then his hand only just avoided squashing a family of scavenging woodlice within the decaying surface, and after observing closely for a moment he began to appreciate the recycling power of these tiny beings. Smiling, he shuffled over to provide them with more room to enjoy their feast.

Jason then took a long and steady look over the undergrowth towards a young deer. Sitting as still as possible and barely daring to breathe, he watched the alert, nervy beast nibble at the saplings, before it sharply lifted its head as if in response to an approaching predator. The animal quickly merged into the shadows, leaving Jason to ponder just how anyone could kill such a wonderful natural creation.

Next to catch his eye was a red squirrel that scampered off down the main trail, before exiting towards the rhododendron where he had hidden the previous day. In this moment he was reminded of his first sighting of these beautiful creatures, when he arrived in Cockington with his dad – *ages* ago, it seemed. Yet why had these animals become so rare? If ever he made it back to Exeter, Jason would look into this.

For some time, everything from bees to buzzards seemed to pass his way – but not one single human. Jason then began to question himself. Had he arrived late? Or even too early? Had Megan taken a dislike to him and now couldn't be bothered? Had he make a prat of himself in trying to impress her with his limited knowledge of birdlife? Had he said something to offend her? Or may it even have been his unusual clothing?

Eventually, after coming to the conclusion that he'd blown it, Jason's coping skills entered another dimension. After all, who really needed a stupid girl? Not him; everything was cool. And anyway, he'd always preferred those with dark hair. Then there was the tribe to save, something *much* more important, and he'd better get on with that.

However, as much as he tried to think and talk and convince himself into an ulterior frame of mind, Jason felt his heart sink.

Then, just as he began to think of something face-saving to tell the tribe, he heard a chaotic cackle from somewhere in the treetops. Was it a magpie, or might it have been Tusher ensconced in the greenery, hand over mouth, having a wicked laugh to himself? There and then, Jason would have kicked the boy's other shin, given the chance.

The frenetic sound soon stopped and was replaced by a purposeful tapping upon a nearby trunk. Jason then imagined that the rhythmic beating was the elf boy relaying a message to his mates, telling them all, with great satisfaction, that Megan hadn't even bothered to turn up.

'Okay, Tush,' he shouted, checking the boughs. 'You've had your fun.'

As things turned out, his eye caught the vibrant green plumage of a woodpecker as it clung to a nearby tree, its colour reminding him of Megan's velvet riding outfit. Yet as much as he wanted to admire the creature, he couldn't.

However, as he spun round to begin the trek back to the village, Jason paused, held his breath, and listened. Could that really be the sound of beating hooves? And was there a horse approaching from the far end of the trail?

He didn't hang around for an answer; a deeper drive from within having already insisted that he sit back on the log. Once there, he was now certain of what he'd heard, and his heart began to flutter. Deep breath in…and slowly out, and in…and out.   It's *cool*, man. Everything's *cool*. He had just enough time to give his teeth a quick polish with his cuff and run his fingers through his hair, before two pricked ears and a flowing white mane emerged from behind a bend on the path.

The young rider was once again cloaked in velvet, and on this occasion the outfit was a shimmering red, several shades deeper than the strawberries Jason had sampled the day before.   As Megan neared on her plodding mount, he caught her radiant smile full in the face and remained fixed to the toppled trunk like one of its tortured branches.

'Do not the men in Exeter stand for a young lady any more?' The girl's smile and gaze prevailed.

Jason sat unmoving for a moment, gawking.   He noticed that she now rode with one leg each side and not side-saddle. 'Oh, er…sorry. I didn't…'

Megan drew to a halt and dismounted. 'I may be a little late. You know how it is for we ladies.'

For fear of appearing to be a complete idiot, Jason worked hard to overcome his inertia, and after sliding to the mouldy forest floor he managed to form at least a few words. 'Yeah, right…no worries. I've only just got here myself.'

Grasping the reins, Megan moved a few steps closer and inhaled deeply, closing her eyes. 'Isn't it beautiful? And cannot you smell that lovely lavender?'

Jason felt his cheeks warm. 'Yeah, it's cool.'

Megan agreed that it *was* cool, although Jason realised that she had missed his own meaning of the word. He let it go, having no wish at this point to complicate matters unnecessarily.

After winding the leather straps around a nearby branch, the girl sat on the log, her black riding boots hanging a little way off the ground, and placed her flat hat to one side. With a gloved hand she then patted the space next to her and invited Jason to sit down. 'The strangest thing happened on my way here,' she began.

Jason could see from the look on her face that she was expecting a prompt. 'Oh, yeah. So what's that, then?'

'I know it sounds silly, but I'm sure that I heard a voice calling out for someone called Tush. Did you hea…?'

'…no, no…I didn't.' Jason then realised that he'd spoken far too soon. 'Hold on…yeah, there was something, but I think it was just the wind, or even those chime things.' As he delivered his response, he found it difficult to look Megan in the eye.

Yet she seemed not to notice his unease. 'Yes, this is a funny old place in here. And I know it is nonsense, but sometimes I feel that these old trees have eyes.'

Jason had to steady himself on the log. 'Yeah, whatever,' were the only stuttering words that followed his nervous burst of laughter.

The girl grinned and nonchalantly placed her hand upon his. She then opened her eyes widely and attempted to speak in a creepy voice. 'Maybe it's those nasty wood sprites.'

Jason forced a smile, but Megan's next suggestion ensured that it was short-lived.

'I was thinking that you could ride with me today,' she said, her eyes excited and innocent.

With his pulse now bounding, Jason took a deep breath to recover his thoughts. 'Can't we just walk around the forest, and I'll show you some of the nice places I've seen?'

'Come now.' Megan stood up. 'Where's your spirit of adventure?' She then leant into Jason's startled face. 'You *can* ride a horse, can't you?'

'*Sure,*' he said after a brief hesitation, again finding it difficult to look her in the eye.

Inwardly he cringed and attempted to dig deep into his past to rekindle his wealth of riding skills. Firstly, there was the experience on Exmouth beach about ten years before. Jason remembered the beast's name – Daisy – and its straw hat with the words, *Kiss Me Quick,* but not much else. Then, a couple of years ago with his mates, he had twice gone on the merry-go-round at the shopping centre in Exeter. That horse was called Dandy. And last year, again with his friends, he had strayed into a field near his home, only to be kicked in the thigh when he ventured too close to its resident pony. He never did find out that one's name, although he remembered calling it something.

They soon walked down the track and stopped at the clearing, where Jason was still holding the reins that Megan had handed to him.

'Are we going to ride here?' he asked.

Megan shook her head and cautiously looked around. 'I don't think my father would take kindly to his sixteen year-old daughter associating with a young man. Particularly, one he does not know.' She pointed to the woods on the other side of the opening. 'Chelston meadow is beyond those trees. Come along...he shan't spy us there.'

Jason was pleased to discover that she and he shared the same age. And with this knowledge, as he walked through this other part of the forest, he wouldn't feel so uneasy with making some subtle enquiries. Indeed, he wouldn't now feel that he was taking advantage in any way, his needs now stemming from somewhere deeper within. Then, having already realised that her world was far removed from his, he reminded himself not to appear surprised with anything that she may say.

'So, how's life in the sticks?' Jason had attempted to sound casual but was rewarded with a long inquisitive look from Megan that seemed to question his sanity. 'Sorry, I mean the countryside,' he then stuttered.

The girl soon smiled again and began by explaining how she didn't really see much of her father. 'He's *far* too busy with the problems of almost single-handedly managing the estate and with the threat of invasion by Napoleon.'

And at last – without the need to arouse suspicion – Jason now had a rough fix on the time period. Once more thinking back to his history lessons, he was now pretty sure that it was early eighteen hundred and something. How *cool* was that?

Megan went on to tell Jason that her time was usually spent at home learning subjects such as French, music, and dancing, mostly from a governess. 'I was taught sewing and embroidery, too,' she said, and beamed with pride as she continued, 'I even make my own riding costumes.' Then her expression changed and she frowned. 'Making costumes and all the rest are somewhat dull, though.' The frown disappeared as quickly as it had come as she concluded: 'But the horses are wonderful…I really love them.'

'So where's your governess now?' Jason asked, now adopting a more sincere tone.

'She has gone…just like almost everyone else who has ever worked for my father.' Megan described how, in recent years, he had been prone to wild mood swings, and how threatened others would feel in his company. 'He can become very angry at times, I fear.'

'And what about the rest of your family?' Jason went on.

Megan paused for a moment, then spoke softly. 'There is no one else. My mother passed away four years ago.'

Jason felt himself stuttering. 'Oh, I'm sorry. How did…?'

The girl raised her gloved hand. 'Let us speak no more of it.' Then walking on again. 'I am just glad that you arrived, Jason. It can be a little lonely around these parts, even with my horses for company.'

The pitch on their voices changed as they approached the edge of the woodland, which eventually yielded to rolling fields with a scattering of slanting, windswept groves. And the criss-crossing of the hedgerows created a tapestry of greens and yellows, interspersed with splashes of newly-ploughed red.

After walking to one of the fields, Megan took the reins from Jason and invited him to climb into the saddle. 'Ride to that old oak at the far side, along the river bank, and then back to me. And be careful; George can be a handful.'

'Yeah, right...no worries.' Jason had convinced himself that there was nothing to this horse riding business. After all, it should only be a case of sitting there with leather straps in his hand and shouting *giddy-up*.

His first effort at clambering onto the shining leather was met with a bemused look from Megan. He had placed his right foot into the left stirrup and had somehow managed to end up facing backwards. The next attempt resulted in him falling straight onto his backside and into a clump of flowering thistles, then staring painfully up to Megan who was trying to suppress a titter.

'Let me help you up,' she said, offering a hand and wiping a tear from her cheek with the other. 'I can only imagine that you haven't ridden for a while.'

Jason was glad for the assistance, and he realised that she was probably being more than kind with her choice of words.

'Let me remind you how to mount properly,' Megan went on.

And so began Jason's first ever riding lesson. His teacher remained patient throughout, calmly demonstrating the correct procedure for ascending to the beast's back.

'Yes, very good, Jason. Left foot into left stirrup...good. Now hold there and swing your right leg over. Fine, but you must learn to relax, because if you are nervous, George will sense it and become edgy, too.'

In the end, and for the first tour of the meadow, Megan held the reins as the horse plodded through the swaying field of buttercups and cornflowers, with Jason clutching his sweaty hands to the pommel as if his life depended upon it.

Then he was led at a leisurely pace past the painfully old oak and alongside the river, its water trickling lazily over lichen covered boulders on its way to the nearby sea.

'So tell me,' said Megan. 'Do you go to school?'

Jason had expected to be on the receiving end of the girl's inquisitive nature sooner rather than later, but nonetheless he still felt a little awkward. 'Yeah...in Exeter...one of the big schools there.'

'How exciting,' Megan continued. 'Do tell me more.'

Jason was beginning to feel increasingly uneasy with the notion of lying, but would there really be any value in telling Megan all about his IT classes? Ultimately, he played safe and told Megan that he studied history, mathematics, science, and French; all of which was true.

'So you speak French?' asked Megan, looking pleased but not surprised. 'That's good, because I need someone with whom to practise.'

Jason listened as her tongue lapsed into something that was way beyond his own level of knowledge, leaving him gaping in disbelief. And although he recognised a few of the words, any meaning completely escaped him. 'Sorry, but I'm a bit rusty at the moment,' he said, looking and sounding sheepish.

Megan grinned. 'Perhaps when you have brushed up on your riding, we can move on to language lessons.'

Jason gave the slightest of nods, before continuing to explain how his parents were now living apart, and that he had come to Torquay to spend the weekend with his father. But no way would he raise the subject of a festival, figuring that in Megan's nineteenth-century Cockington such an event would seem very odd. He also had to be careful when it came to discussing his interests, staying well clear of any mention of football and computers. Instead, he played safe with climbing trees and walking.

A short time later, Jason felt more relaxed and had enough confidence to release one hand at a time from the pommel to dry his sticky palms on his jeans. He saw Megan look to him at this point.

'I can see that you're regaining your confidence,' she said. 'Here, you may take these now.' Coming to a stop, she handed the leather straps to a reluctant Jason.

'Now, little fingers under there and curl the others around...that's it. And then turn your hand so as your thumb is on top.'

As Megan delivered her patient instruction she manipulated Jason's fingers into the correct position, and before long his white knuckles were facing forward. 'No need to hold so tightly,' she added, prompting Jason to release some of the tension in the reins.

None of his schoolteachers had ever demonstrated such a calm and helpful manner. On the contrary, some of them made Jason feel like a complete idiot when he struggled to grasp any new knowledge. Indeed, the only person that he could think of that came anywhere close was his dad and, if only for a brief moment, realised how much he missed him – not so much now, but certainly in his own time.

He continued with his equestrian tuition, covering the basics of the correct sitting position, walking and trotting, turning, slowing and halting; and finally, dismounting. He also learned how best to praise and encourage the powerful beast using voice, hand, and foot commands.

By the end of the session Jason had managed to ride independently, albeit slowly, around the field. However, Megan didn't match the smile that he displayed on returning.

'That's very good,' she said, 'but I really should think about going home now. I don't want my father to come looking for me.'

Jason had no idea of the time, but he reckoned that they must have spent at least a couple of hours with each other. 'Can't we just stay a little longer?' he pleaded. 'Surely, your dad won't mind that much.'

Megan sighed. 'You don't know him like I do, or how he worries when I'm out riding.' Swapping places with Jason she then pointed to the nearby woods. 'If you go through there you'll come to the clearing, and then to the combe.'

'And what about you?' asked Jason as he saw Megan turning the horse to face the other way.

She smiled. 'I am taking a short cut over the next field.'

Jason did his best to disguise the anxiety in his voice. 'But can I see you again?'

The girl laughed. 'You are so funny, how could I refuse such an offer? Tomorrow…same time, same place.'

As soon as Jason had nodded, his friend delivered a sharp kick into the horse's sides, and before long they had trotted across the meadow and disappeared around a hummock. And for some time he stood knee-deep in a rippling carpet of blue and yellow, not wanting to move, eyes closed, wishing for the moment and feelings to last forever.

Once more there was a spring in his step as he eventually moved along the track and into the clearing. However, in the middle of the sun-drenched expanse he lifted his distracted head just in time to spot two figures, one of them bearded, staggering arm-in-arm next to the woodland that lined the dell. Just who were they? Jason held his breath and crouched down on the grass, hoping that he wouldn't be spotted.

The rough characters, humans younger looking than his dad, were singing and heading in the direction of the manor house. They stopped occasionally to peer into the forest as though looking for something, and as much as he tried to tap into their mutterings in the breeze, they were too slurred in their speech to make out.

Jason watched on as they exchanged some sort of large bottle between them, each taking a turn at placing it upon his shoulder and having what looked like a long drink of something or other. These men were drunk, he reasoned, and he would wait until they had passed before crossing the clearing.

Some time had elapsed before he felt safe enough to dash over the grass and jump over a mass of brambles and into the woods. Landing on the other side, he thought that he heard a distant shout; something like, '*Oi...you there*,' followed by nothing more than birdsong as he moved deeper into the dell.

Once more on Dumni land and feeling safer, his thoughts began to return to its resident tribe. Just what message of hope would he bring to them? He would have to sit down for a while to instil some sort of order to his scrambled thoughts.

Later in the afternoon, when he eventually arrived back at the main hamlet, Jason could see that the preparations were continuing for the change of leader. A few of the tribe remained at the central fireside, singing and playing an unusual array of musical instruments, whilst others mobbed him like he was some sort of returning superhero.

Mans bustled to the front of the crowd and was the first to speak. 'We pray that the news is good,' he said, stretching up to place a welcome hand on Jason's shoulder.

However, long before Jason had reached the hamlet he realised that, as far as saving the Dumni was concerned, no headway had been made. Indeed, the only real progress that he could think of was in his riding skills – and in winning the affection of a very attractive girl. Even so, for fear of being perceived as a total failure, he felt obliged to give the tribe something positive in return. 'I've befriended the earl's daughter and made some enquiries over her father.' Then looking to the king. 'I don't think you have anything to fear from Megan, and so you must decide whether or not the time has come for me to tell her of the Dumni.'

But his attempts at describing how kind she had seemed were quickly drowned out by the concerned chatter that his last statement had caused.

'First you,' shouted one of the older men standing next to Mans, 'then the maid. And before us know it, every giant in the world will descend upon us. So I says us fight, and 'tis best that you be gone, too.'

'Aye,' several others cried in agreement. And very soon the whole village had descended into a squabbling mass, which continued for some time until the king raised his hands high above his head.

'*Enough*,' Mans shouted, and almost immediately the scene fell silent; including the wildlife, it seemed. For a few moments the king surveyed the expectant faces of his subjects, before delivering his judgement. 'My reign may be drawing to an end, but until that moment I alone shall have the final say in this matter.' Then turning to the man who had asked for war. 'I admire your bravery, my warrior friend, but we would surely all perish in any conflict.' He concluded by addressing Jason. 'You said that you wished to do things on your own. And with that in mind it is only right for you to determine the correct path to take.'

Jason nodded, but with time quickly running out he had no real choice in the matter. After a short delay and with a growing awareness of the risks to the tribe and to himself, he told everyone of his intention to meet Megan at the same time the next day, when he would tell her of the existence of the Dumni. 'And let's hope she can persuade her father to help you because, whether you like it or not, I think he's the only one who can.'

This had been one of the longest, and at times most enjoyable, days in Jason's life. The evening sun may still have been shining, but he would go to bed to make up for the previous night's disastrous sleep and rise early to prepare for the anticipated difficult day that lay ahead. Except, as he walked alone and away from the muttering crowd towards Mans's cottage, he could never have imagined how tough that day would be...

Chapter Eight

'*Come on*, Jason. It's time to go.' This was the third time that he'd heard these soft words probing his sleepy head, and on each occasion he'd responded by pressing his hands to his ears and turning the other way. Well, it *was* Saturday and, with no school, just what was his mother playing at? She may have sounded somewhat younger and less forceful than usual, but why couldn't she just leave him to have a long lie-in?

The next voice to disturb him penetrated deeper and was accompanied by a strong shake to his shoulder. 'Time runs short...you must rouse yourself...*now.*' Was that his dad trying to wrench him from his bed? And were his parents really back together again?

Lifting his heavy eyelids, a few moments had elapsed before Jason realised that the dark wooden beams on the ceiling didn't belong to his house in Exeter. An instant later he bolted upright and looked hazily into the king's eyes. 'Sorry, I...' He then shot up to his feet and, in a panic, grabbed the sleeve on Mans's robe. 'What's the time? Tell me I'm not late.'

He then heard how Ethera had attempted several times to waken him up and that, as late morning had passed without success, the king himself had been called in to assist in the matter.

Jason thanked them, before grabbing a quick drink of water. He was soon halfway out the door, zipping up his jacket and trying to do something with his morning hair, when he turned back to father and daughter. 'Well...this is it. Let's just hope I get there in time.'

The speedy exit seemed to catch almost everyone by surprise as, on this occasion, only a handful of individuals had appeared to see him off. Nevertheless, they wished him well.

Out of puff and still clearing his gritty eyes, Jason arrived at the meeting place. The sun's high angle informed him that he was running late, and he was relieved to find Megan perched upon the log, swinging her booted legs back and forth; impatiently, it seemed.

'So, the men from Exeter like to keep a lady waiting, do they?' She only kept her face straight for a short moment, but it was enough to concern Jason.

'Sorry,' he said, half covering his mouth and looking down. 'I was helping my dad with something.'

'Not to worry.' With the smile now restored to the girl's face, she hopped down from the log. 'So, shall we take George to the meadow again?'

Jason looked to her red velvet riding outfit, and then over to the horse who appeared to be happily chomping on the wild flowers at the side of the trail. However, as much as he really wanted to climb upon the inviting saddle, he knew that he had other business to attend to. 'Sorry, Megan. I, er...I'm quite sore from that fall in the field yesterday.' In fact, he did have some pain in his lower back and so didn't feel too bad with telling her this.

'Oh, that's a pity. For you did very well.' Megan came closer and gazed into his eyes. 'So, what shall we do instead?'

Jason couldn't have wished for a better question. 'Can't we just spend some time in here today? I'd like to show you a thing or two.'

Megan appeared to consider the suggestion for a moment, before slowly nodding her head. 'Very well, Jason. To which part of the haunted combe are you going to take me?'

He sensed an element of teasing in her wide eyes and tone of voice. Jason then invited her to sit once again on the log, saying that he had something that she should hear.

Once atop and swinging her legs as she'd done before, Megan was the first to speak. 'Before we go any further, I must tell you something.' She went on to say how her father had been unhappy with her late arrival home the previous day, and that she would have to be more mindful of the time on this occasion. 'He even sent the two stable lads out to search for me,' she concluded.

Jason nodded and told Megan of the two drunken men that he'd seen walking towards the manor house.

'Yes,' she replied. 'They're the only two workers remaining on the estate. They live in the old weaver's cottage, and they're for ever drinking that horrible cider that father gives them.' She then leaned closer to Jason.

'So, what *is* on your mind? For I can see that something vexes you.'

'What?'

'You sound troubled; as though you have the weight of the world upon your shoulders.'

Only then did Jason become aware of the tension in his brow and the moisture on his hot palms. 'I'm all right, really. I just wanted to tell you something, that's all. And I was afraid that you wouldn't believe me.'

Megan placed her hand upon his and gazed into Jason's eyes. 'I promise that I *will* believe you...no matter what you may say.'

Noticing her sincere look, he then said: 'Do you remember telling me that you saw the wind chimes? You know, those things hanging from the trees.'

'Yes, I recall.'

Jason looked directly into Megan's eyes and maintained his serious manner. 'So how do you think they got there?'

There was a short delay before Megan attempted to answer. 'I've never really given it a thought,' she said, now frowning. 'I can only suppose that children must have made them a long time ago.'

The moment had arrived for Jason to take Megan's hand for the first time, and she seemed relaxed with the gesture. 'What if I told you that those chimes were made by elves who still live in this forest?'

Their hands remained joined as he awaited her response. And this time the delay was more prolonged.

'You're very funny,' Megan said eventually, 'and that's what I like most about you.' She went on to cite his supposed knowledge of bird song, and laughed when she recalled that he had actually mixed up those of robins and blackbirds. She also reminded him of the comical horse riding capers, before returning to his question. 'Actually, I think it's a wonderful tale. Do you have any more?'

Jason grimaced. He realised that he now had a battle on his hands and would have to employ more drastic measures. 'Okay, then. How would you feel if I told you I was from the future?'

Megan immediately erupted into loud laughter, and she recovered only after a long moment. 'And is that from any particular time period?' she managed, while still trying to regain her breath.

Jason remained unsmiling and produced something from his jeans' pocket. 'From the year two thousand and eight, to be precise.' He handed a piece of paper to Megan, who held it in her free hand.

After studying the printed note for a few moments, she released her other hand from Jason's. 'I see a picture of a man who shall not be born for another four years. Who is he?' By this time her smile had abandoned her.

Jason looked to the back of the ten-pound note. 'His name's Charles Darwin.' He went on to explain that this man was – or would become – one of the world's greatest ever scientists.

Megan focused on the other side of the note, as well as a coin that Jason had subsequently given to her. 'And Queen Elizabeth?'

'Still on the throne, last I checked.' Amongst other things, Jason then told her about the Duke of Wellington and Lord Nelson, and of their decisive victories over the French. '...so you can tell your father that in the end Napoleon will be defeated.'

The girl grimaced and jumped to the forest floor. 'I think I had better go home now. I just remembered that I have a few chores to attend to.' Megan very quickly ran to her waiting horse and positioned one foot in the stirrup.

However, just as she went to mount, Jason darted over and placed his hand on her shoulder.

'I promise you have nothing to worry about,' he said. 'And I know it sounds crazy, but you must believe me.' Then easing his grip. 'No...more than that, I *need* you to believe me...and so do hundreds of others. *Please*, Megan, because many lives could be lost if you don't.'

Following a short hesitation, Megan stood on the rough grass, reins in hand. 'So there are little people living in here, are there? Well, in that case, you had better advise them to move on, because my father told me this morning that he is selling this part of the estate, and that all the trees in this combe are to be removed to make room for new pasture.'

Jason's eyebrows immediately shot up. This was news indeed, and it made a big difference to his mission. He had already reasoned that her meeting the Dumni was unavoidable, and what he'd just heard underlined how absolutely essential it would be if he were to have any chance of saving the tribe and returning home. 'Why don't you, *yourself*, tell them of your father's plans,' he asked.

For a long moment Megan looked into Jason's unblinking eyes, appearing to consider the request. 'Very well,' she said eventually. 'Take me to these *pixies*. For, as far as I am concerned, seeing is believing.'

With Megan holding George's reins they began the long walk to the main hamlet. On the way, Jason was able to provide her with a more detailed history of his experiences over the past few days, beginning with the trip to Cockington on his sixteenth birthday, and ending with the current state of affairs. For a long time the conversation was one way; Megan listening without interruption throughout Jason's account, which included a mention of the reclusive owner of the manor who was behind the midsummer festival. When he had finished, she once again slipped her hand into his.

'What you say belongs only in a fairy tale.' Twice more Megan asked him to recount his story, and each time she appeared utterly bewildered by what she heard.

However, no matter how much Jason assured her that he was telling the truth, he could see from Megan's continual frown that she remained sceptical.

Twisting through the main trail and nearing the hamlet, George became increasingly agitated and began to resist any further movement, prompting Megan to intervene.

Jason watched with fascination as she then whispered a few words into his ear, until the animal eventually settled and continued his forward plod.

'We are not the only ones here, I fear,' Megan said, scanning the surrounding greenery with suspicious eyes. 'George is *never* wrong.'

And even if the horse was right, Jason knew that Megan would see nothing out of the ordinary lurking in the shimmering leaves. However, for the first time it now seemed that she was beginning to question her own convictions.

As the track eventually opened into the clearing that housed the village, Jason wasn't surprised to find most of its inhabitants standing and waiting for their arrival. He just knew that the Dumni scouting system would have relayed a running commentary of events to the hamlet from a long way off.

And there the little people remained; quiet, motionless and gaping, as if mesmerised with the presence before them. Megan, too, it seemed could do nothing but gawk at the beings gathered in front of her, and she appeared even not to notice George's anxious whinnies.

Jason squeezed her hand gently, and after detecting the merest of nods he slowly led her over to Mans who stood at the head of the welcoming party. Only, as they neared the silent group, Jason noticed that their attention – in particular that of the younger tribal members – was focused not upon the humans, but towards the animal at the end of the reins.

Moving closer still, a few of the elves could be seen to back off, as if their curiosity and fascination had been overcome with terror. Sensing this, Jason raised his hand. 'Don't worry, my friends.' Then patting the horse's neck. 'George won't do you any harm.'

His words and actions appeared to allay their fears as, one by one, the Dumni moved ever nearer. Soon both groups had come together, and with Megan now looking down into the eyes of the bare-footed elder dressed in the red robe, Jason began the introductions.

'This is Mans, King of the Dumni,' he said.

As the tribal leader held out his hand, Megan released the reins and curtsied.

'This is indeed an honour, Your Majesty,' she said, her voice a little shaky as she held the king's small hand.

'The honour is all mine, Megan.' Mans then looked towards the horse. 'And never before have we been so close to such a beautiful beast as this. Maybe we can get to know George better than we do.'

Megan nodded and smiled. 'It would be a pleasure.' Soon she was chattering softly into the animal's attentive ears, before turning back to the king. 'Once he has had a drink and rested, George has agreed to give some rides to the children, if that is all right with you.'

The king accepted the offer and invited Megan and Jason into his cottage where, at the table in the main chamber, Ethera, Lus, and Tusher joined them. Over some water and fruit they were soon well acquainted, and then it was down to business.

Mans began by providing Megan with a history of the Dumni, from ancient times when they ruled over vast areas of unspoiled woodland, up to their present day difficulties.

The girl reciprocated by offering an account of events in the year eighteen hundred and five, which included a description of family life in Cockington estate, her father's plans for the forest, and something that was most concerning for everyone in Britain – the much dreaded and inevitable French invasion.

As for Jason, he was struck by the strange irony of the situation. Here were two distinct races of people, both fearing imminent destruction by alien forces, and each seemingly powerless to help themselves.

Following the day's unexpected revelations, Megan insisted on passing the afternoon with the tribe, which she claimed would help her in planning how best to approach the subject of the Dumni with her father.

As Jason began to show her around the village, he noticed how quickly she had shrugged off her bewilderment and was once again brimming with confidence. In her elegant clothing, Megan now reminded him of a young princess on a royal visit, who appeared to delight in chatting informally with the lines of villagers. Also, he realised that for the woodlanders, this would have been the very first time that any of them had ever seen a female human being, and an ogre she certainly was not. Little wonder, therefore, that she had small groups following her around, with some of the younger ones even daring to touch her hand as though checking that she was real.

Soon it seemed that she had won the hearts of everyone within the hamlet, and at the end of the tour one of the infants approached her and offered a posy of flowers. Megan was told that they were called fairies' basins, although Jason recognised them as buttercups. This brought a tear to Megan's eye and she knelt down to hug the child. After doing so and drying her reddened cheeks, she then looked to the others. 'I promise that I shall do all that I can to help you.'

After eventually prising Megan away from the giggling children, Jason could hear screams and wild laughter – and he soon discovered the cause. A short distance away stood Tusher upon the saddle like some sort of circus act, reins in hand, trotting around the dusty earth in small circles, with an excited looking audience of his friends egging him on.

'Don't worry, Megan,' said Jason. 'I'll put a stop to this carry on.' He began to make his way over with purpose in his stride but was soon halted by Megan's call.

'No, Jason,' she said. 'If George does not like something he would not allow it. And I can see that the Dumni have a natural talent.'

Tusher and the horse eventually came to a halt as Jason and Megan reached them.

The girl then offered a round of applause. 'Wonderful riding, I should say.'

The elf boy blushed. ''Tis nothing, really. Me and George just had a little chat, and he told me what to do.'

Megan raised her eyebrows. 'And do you make a habit of speaking with animals?'

Tusher smiled and looked to his band of green-shawled friends. 'Us all do. Ain't that right, lads?'

With George appearing so relaxed with the elfin company, and with Tusher looking to be in control of things, they were left to get on with the show.

In the meantime, Jason escorted Megan to the bottom of a nearby rope ladder. It hung from a sturdy oak bough and ascended a fair height into a tree house, from where they could watch the ongoing antics of George with his new friends. They were soon crouched within, fingers entwined, and gazing warmly into each other's eyes.

'In my dreams alone,' said Megan, 'have I imagined anything as beautiful as this day.' With her free hand, she then gently stroked Jason's cheek.

In this moment Jason believed that he could fly, and perhaps if she were to hold his hand tightly enough, Megan could soar over the trees with him.

Much later, as the sun neared the treetops, the time had arrived for Jason to escort Megan back through the forest. And the farewell turned out to be the longest that he had ever experienced, as Megan made a point of chatting to almost everyone before she would go. The last person she spoke with was Mans.

'I'm sure that I can charm my father into helping,' she said, smiling. Then sounding less certain. 'But you do realise that he shall have to see all of this for himself.'

As Mans grimaced, Jason placed a hand upon the king's shoulder, and said: 'It's the only way, because sooner or later we must trust him. And with it being midsummer tomorrow, we've got to do something *now*.'

Following a long deliberation, the king produced a cautious nod of his head. 'Maybe we have been wrong to assume that all humans are alike. For I have seen a kindness and warmth in the only two that I have yet encountered.' He smiled towards Jason and Megan as he said so. 'And I can only pray that the man who claims these lands possesses those same talents.'

Between them the final plan was soon agreed. Megan would somehow coerce her father into the dell, where they would meet up with Jason and be taken to the king's village to begin negotiations.

Strolling back through the snaking forest trail, Jason and Megan locked arms, leaving George to trudge along behind with no one to hold the reins. Around halfway into the journey, Jason suggested that they should stop for a rest and a snack. And knowing that they were close to the ideal spot, he veered off the main path and paused at the top of a densely wooded incline.

Megan looked around at the trees. 'It sounds like a storm is brewing, yet I see no movement in the leaves.'

Jason secured the horse's reins to a nearby branch and led Megan down through the undergrowth where, at times, the gradient was so steep that they both lost their footing in the soft humus. And after much giggling and teasing, they reached a level patch of tall ferns where they waited to regain their breath.

'So tell me, Jason. Why have you brought me all the way down here?' Megan's voice only just managed to overcome the nearby rushing din.

He smiled and pointed to a moss covered rocky ledge. 'Go and stand over there.'

She did so, and only after a long moment did she turn back with her eyes and mouth wide.

Rejoining her and holding Megan's hand, they both sat down speechless, as if enchanted by the natural beauty that now surrounded them.

At the top of the shady gorge, the dark water began its long descent from within the tangled roots of the forest floor. Rushing past the spectators on the ledge, the speed of the fall sheered the torrent into a multitude of silvery strands and pearly drops, before crashing into a mist enshrouded frothy pool far below.

For Jason the scene was like something from a tropical rain forest – without the heat. In fact, he could only imagine that, for most of the year, this ravine had never seen much direct sunlight; at best receiving only a daytime twilight and the pitch black of night.

For a while they sat in silence, breathing the cool moist air, until eventually Megan lay back onto the mossy slab and rested on her elbows.

'This is just how I would imagine paradise to be.' She then patted the area next to her and invited Jason to join her. 'I want you to tell me again about life in the twenty-first century.'

Jason agreed and after producing some soft fruit from his backpack, rested next to Megan. While they snacked, he told her more of his own home life and of the world in general. However, after a short time he noticed the way in which she was gazing into his eyes; distant, as if under a spell. And as he continued to speak, he began to realise that she wasn't actually paying any attention to what he was saying. 'You all right?' he asked, taking her hand in his.

There returned a brief silence, before Megan eventually leaned into the side of his face. 'It matters not that you come from another world; you are still my little summer breeze.' She smiled and began to speak to him in French for a moment, as though toying.

Jason didn't quite follow everything that she said, but he did understand her final words, '*Je t'aime*,' before she planted a soft kiss on his cheek.

Grinning and with her eyes closed, Megan lay on her back as if immersed in things pleasant. She then ran her fingers through her hair and placed her hands behind her head.

Rolling onto his side, Jason rested upon one arm and gazed down into Megan's flawless face. 'What are you thinking about now?' he asked, smiling.

The girl kept her eyes closed and took a deep breath. 'Just dreaming of songs to sing and dances to dance.'

Jason could find no more words to offer. Instead, he would caress her rosy cheek and pale neck with his berry-stained fingers; except, as he moved to do so, and with Megan seemingly expectant, he heard a call from a little way up the slope.

'Ah...I sees a lover boy in these here woods.' The voice was loud, male, and slurred, and it was quickly followed by another from within a nearby shrub.

'Aye...and just about to have his wicked way with a helpless maid.'

Jason didn't recognise the voices and was soon helping Megan to her feet. Squinting up, he saw a rough looking man stumbling down the steep slope towards the ledge, carrying a scythe. Then someone else emerged from the foliage close to the flattened ferns; similarly equipped, but also clutching a loaded crossbow.

And only when they approached to within a few paces and had stopped, did Jason realise that he'd seen these men before. However, before he could say anything Megan had taken a step forward.

'What is the meaning of this outrage?' she demanded of the man now swigging the golden contents from a clear bottle.

The bearded character swayed a little and answered through blackened teeth. 'Well, you see, My Lady. Your father gave me and Ball the job of finding what you was up to.' He then passed the drink to his stubble-faced companion.

Megan's face was turning red. 'How *dare* you come spying upon me,' she shouted.

Ball, the shorter of the men and with the crossbow at his side, then offered his view. 'Aye, but for five barrels of scrumpy I thinks me and Beckford would walk through hell itself.'

Megan's voice was still raised. 'Well, as you can see, I'm perfectly all right. So I would suggest that you go back to your cot and come to your senses.'

Both men laughed; menacingly, it seemed to Jason.

''Tisn't as easy as that, My Lady,' said Beckford. 'Because we was told to bring you home with us...no matter what.'

Megan glowered. 'Well, I *was* on my way home before you two fools appeared. So just you move along and I shall follow soon afterwards.'

''Fraid not,' said Ball, shaking his head. 'We haves to take you there. *Now.*'

'I don't think the lady wants to go.' Jason then moved to stand between the men and Megan with his arms folded and his chin thrust forward. However, even though he had tried to sound composed, there appeared a slight quiver in his voice, and he noticed the men sizing up his trainers, jeans, and zip-up hooded top.

'Just what do we haves here, then?' asked Beckford. 'For them clothes ain't from these parts.'

'Aye,' added Ball. 'And Lady Megan were speaking to him in a strange tongue.'

The bearded man sniggered and held his scythe aloft. 'Well, well, well. We *was* just going to scare you off, but it looks like we've got ourselves one of they French spies, don't you think, Ball?'

'Oh, I don't knows, Beckford. Ain't they supposed to be short and hairy with curly tails?'

'What are you talking about?' demanded Jason. 'I'm from Exeter.'

The shorter of the men looked to Megan. 'You may be able to fool this here young lady.' He then aimed his crossbow into Jason's face. 'But we was told to look out for the likes of you. Coming over here to spread your revolution and all.'

Megan pushed to the front once more. 'This is ludicrous. Jason is as English as I am, and I demand that you leave us alone.'

Ball laughed. 'With a hundred guineas reward for catching one of they, we is going nowheres.'

'You shall not lay a solitary finger upon him,' the girl persisted, 'for he has given to me important news to pass to my father.'

Beckford nodded. 'I'm sure he has, and before we knows it our own dear King George will be losing his head. So I tells you, My Lady, to stand aside and let us save you from this Frenchie.'

'Aye,' added Ball. ''Tis for your own good.'

As Jason stood behind Megan, the smell of sweet damp woodland had been overcome with that of stale apples and alcohol. He reckoned that he was taller than these two drunks and could perhaps look after himself. Then again, they looked strong and well-made and, furthermore, he didn't fancy an encounter with a sharp blade or with a speeding bolt.

'Listen guys,' he said. 'I do have something important to tell the earl, but Megan was going to speak to him first.'

'So,' said Beckford, 'getting an innocent maid to do your dirty work for you. And just what be it you want to say to His Lordship?'

Following a long pause and a pleading stare from Megan, Jason said: 'I can't tell you; it's a secret.'

'Well, there you go,' said Ball, who walked closer and raised his weapon. 'You'm a spy, for sure. Now put them grubby paws where I can sees them.'

Raising his hands, Jason was stunned with the speed of Megan's actions. In a split moment she had thrust herself forward, knocked the crossbow from Ball's hand, and sent the stocky figure tumbling into a bed of feathered fronds.

As the man groaned within the mangled ferns, his companion brandished his own scythe. 'Now don't be daft, My Lady. We don't wants to do this the hard way.'

Jason immediately lifted his hands over his head. 'Okay, then. Take me, but leave Megan alone.'

However, as Beckford lowered his blade, Jason dashed towards the burly figure, bowled him over with his shoulder, and began to grapple with the man on the ground.

Megan, too, joined in the fracas, and with Ball still languishing within the undergrowth, the three figures began to scrap upon the ledge.

There followed a short and frantic period of screaming, heaving, and panting, before Jason and Beckford paused to stare at one another's bloodied faces with wide, disbelieving eyes. The tight grip that they had on each other's clothing was soon relaxed, as almost simultaneously they peered down into the sheer drop.

Some way below in the mottled shade, a crumpled figure lay motionless. The hair was now tinged with red, and the pool now featured a foaming pink. Even the rising mist seemed tainted.

'Megan,' yelled Jason, before jumping to his feet to find a safer route down to where she lay. And very shortly he reached the spot where the girl remained unmoving, face down in the water.

The pool now matched the colour of Megan's dress, and the first thing that Jason did was to roll her away from the water and to make sure that she was breathing.

As he cradled her wounded head in his arms, he held his ear over her gaping mouth, but all that he could hear was a faint gurgle, nothing more. With her flaccid arms resting upon the wet rocks, he gave her a gentle shake. 'Megan...please say something...tell me you're all right.' The salt from a mixture of blood, sweat, and tears filled his mouth as he caressed her cold, anaemic cheek. 'Please be all right...plea...'

Just then he felt a heavy thud on the side of his head, keeling him over into the stream. As he managed to sit up in the water and nurse his aching temple, Jason saw the two men standing over Megan, both of them shaking their heads and muttering. Then they turned to him.

'You've done it now,' said Beckford, rubbing the knuckles on his shovel-like hand.

'And when the earl hears what you did, you'll wish you was already dead,' continued Ball, who then aimed the crossbow at Jason's chest. 'Now, *get up.*'

The teenager was in no frame of mind to argue. 'Let's forget about who's to blame. Megan needs help...and quick.' He noticed the men look to the bundled red heap, and then to each other, before they rested their eyes upon him.

''Tis too late for that now, Frenchie.' Ball approached with his crossbow. 'And anyway, you'd better worry about what be in store for you, ain't that right, Beckford?' Both men began to laugh and shared another drink.

Jason was then forced up the bank to the patch of forest where George had been left. Behind him, Ball remained at a safe distance, but with the crossbow well within firing range. In front, Beckford supported the limp figure of Megan, her arms and legs furrowing through the leaf mould.

Along the way, Jason began to think, but not about escape…no way was he leaving Megan. Why had the little people not heard all the commotion and come to their rescue? Surely, one of them must have sensed something of the racket. Then again, everything had happened deep within a narrow ravine, and perhaps all the shouting had been contained within or drowned out by the cascading waters. In the end, these were the only explanations that he could think of.

Yet maybe, when he reached the top, he could call for help or even attempt the blackbird's distress call. But the latter option was soon dropped as he had forgotten how to do it, and any notion of shouting out was discounted as he stood breathless next to the horse and heard Beckford say to Ball: 'One word…and let him have it between the eyes.'

Megan's broken body was then slung like an animal's carcass over George's saddle. The horse whinnied loudly, but the most that Jason dared to do was to pat the animal's neck, which eventually seemed to ease its distress.

Trudging through the dappled evening shade, the journey back to the manor began. Beckford once again led the way, hacking with his scythe in one hand and yanking George's reins with the other. Staggering at the rear, clutching his weapon, bottle at his mouth, and with the curved blade attached to the thick leather belt, came Ball.

Jason remained to the side of the horse, with Megan's dripping hair and flailing arms within touching distance. And looking at her red matted scalp, he was beginning to think that he *had* been to blame for her fall after all, and he now wished that he had been the one to plummet into the pool.

Walking along, and for just a brief moment, he managed to hold Megan's slender hand and to give it a gentle squeeze. Then moving his fingers a little higher towards her wrist, he was sure that he could detect a pulse. It felt rapid and weak, but it was a sure sign that she lived, at least for the moment. 'I'm sorry, Megan,' he whispered, feeling only partially relieved. 'I'll look after you. I promise.'

At every opportunity Jason discreetly caressed the back of her hand in some hopeful attempt to reassure her, and himself, that things would be all right. And even when he approached the pillared doorway of the manor, Jason could think of nothing but the welfare of the girl who was strewn over the leather saddle.

From the grand building, which was now beginning to eclipse the evening sun, Jason noticed someone emerge from the entrance. Waiting there for only a brief moment, a man then raced into the clearing, past

Beckford as if he didn't exist, and straight to the unmoving pile of redness. It seemed that, in his state of panic, he didn't even notice Jason standing nearby and had soon lifted the girl from the saddle to hold her in his arms. 'No...no...please, God. Please, not Megan.' There he remained for a long moment, talking to the blood-stained bundle next to his chest, demanding that she open her eyes. However, she did not, and with a tear falling from his cheek he turned to his stable lads, where his tone suddenly changed. 'What the hell have you done to my daughter?'

Megan's father didn't appear quite as Jason had expected. He had prepared himself for a meeting with someone in a white curly wig, sporting a pale powdered face, and wearing tights. Yet this figure, he noticed, had short-cropped, dark wavy hair, a high white collar, and a red cravat. Also, instead of tights, he wore dark trousers tucked into knee-length leather boots.

Beckford shook his head. ''Tisn't as you think, My Lord.' Then pointing to Jason. 'This here Frenchie be the one who did it.' He went on to provide a colourful confabulation of events, claiming that Jason had attacked Megan after she had refused to conspire with him, before throwing her into the ravine. As he made himself out to be her saviour, Beckford was all the while backed up by his companion. And by the time they had finished their story, Jason felt like he'd already been tried and convicted.

With Megan still in his arms, the earl approached him. 'If I had a free hand I would surely run you through.' Then turning to the stable lads. 'Take this dirty foreigner to the stable,' he shouted, ' and tie him up until I decide what to do with him.'

'I...' Jason felt a sharp blow in his lower back as the earl carried Megan to the front door.

'Get yourself moving, *Monshoor*,' demanded Ball, with a firm grip on his crossbow. 'And keep your mouth shut.'

Now silenced, Jason trudged behind Beckford and George and past a parked open-top carriage. Its polished leather seat reminded him of the one that he'd sat upon at the Cockington festival, but he had no time to dwell on the matter as he was quickly shown into a dingy stable complete with the fresh, but inoffensive, smell of horse manure.

He was soon re-introduced to the powerful hands of the bearded stable lad, as the drunken figure bound his wrists and ankles with rope. A length of the same material was used as a gag, before he received a parting slap to the face and was tossed to the cobbled floor.

'And don't gets too settled,' said Beckford, 'for His Lordship will pay you another visit this evening, for sure. And it won't be for a good night kiss, neithers.' He and his companion then filled a couple of bottles from a nearby barrel, before leaving and bolting the door behind them.

Jason listened to their fading laughter as he managed to rock himself up to a sitting position with his hands behind him. Looking up a ladder to the loft area, he noticed a huge mound of hay. Perhaps he could climb upon it, through one of the skylights in the high-pitched ceiling, and out onto the roof. It looked like the only means of escape. Then again, even if he could, did he really want to return to the dell? Megan was surely somewhere nearby, and perhaps he could find her and help. Maybe he could even reach the earl and tell him what had really happened that day, and of the Dumni.

For some time he attempted to wriggle free, but Jason was soon lying back, breathless, on a pile of musty straw in the ground level. Never before had he known such darkness as, quite literally, he could now see nothing at all, and he began to realise just how the world must have seemed to Ethera. His loneliness would have been every bit as profound, if it wasn't for the occasional scurrying rodent or soft whinny from George and the other horses.

As exhausted as he felt, and as much as he wanted to close his eyes, Jason couldn't. His wrists and ankles had been bound so tightly that they burned to the bone, and it felt as if the rope that straddled his mouth was cutting into his cheeks like a hot cheese wire through cheddar.

The night wore painfully on, and the silvery light that had begun to sift through the windows and cracks and vents reminded him – like he needed it – of another matter. Tomorrow night the moon would be full, by which time he should have saved the tribe.

In his mind he then tried to forge a path between lying helpless on a stinking floor, and returning as a reluctant hero to the dell. However, rolling over to the bolted entrance was about as far as his imagination would stretch, and Jason's heart sank. Things couldn't be much worse, could they?

Just as Jason was thinking this, he detected some activity from outside the stable door, as though someone was undoing the bolt. Sitting up once again and peering through the thin white shafts amid the blackness, the timbered door was pulled open. At first he felt a little relieved that he wasn't facing the drunken stable lads, yet the ghostly outline and silence that he encountered proved to be more unnerving.

The man's muteness prevailed as he walked slowly into the building, leaving the door open behind him. Now with the passage of copious moonlight into the stable, Jason was able to watch the figure pace up and down in his squeaking boots, hand to the side of his head, as if contemplating his next move.

Even if Jason hadn't been gagged, he would have chosen to say nothing at this time. This man was no longer burdened with his daughter's stricken body, and the teenager remembered what the earl had said about using his sword, which now swung ominously from his belt in the silvery light.

Only after a long moment did Megan's father stop his posturing, prompting Jason to back off, as best he could, deeper into the stable. When he could retreat no more he found his back supported by a stone wall, with his heart hammering at his chest, demanding to leave his body.

As the earl edged closer, his eyes were fixed upon the trembling teenager. 'Have you touched Megan?' he said. And even though the man's voice was soft, it was accompanied by his hand taking a tight hold on the sword's handle.

Jason now wanted to tell him everything, but all that he produced was a few guttural croaks through the tight gag.

The earl shook his head. 'Perhaps your English is limited, and you did not understand. So I shall put it another way.' He withdrew his sword from its scabbard, leaned into Jason's terrified face with intent upon his own furrowed brow, and shouted through gritted teeth. '*Avez-vous touché ma fille?*'

Jason didn't need the French version, having understood the question the first time. However, as Megan's father glared upon him, Jason's attention was diverted elsewhere. There was something about the earl's eyes and his voice that reminded him of someone else, but he couldn't think who it was. And as he scoured the depths of his mind, the tantalising memory slipped away like a fading dream.

'The physician has told me that my daughter is dying, yet you have the nerve to look me in the face?' The earl moved the point of the gleaming white blade close to Jason's throat. 'This is your final chance…*did you touch her?*'

Jason froze, and even though he now knew what the earl was really asking, not the merest sound could he utter. Indeed, the only response that he produced was a tear from his unblinking eyes and the slightest of shakes with his head.

The earl then raised the sword over his head, where he held it quivering in his hand, and Jason snapped his eyes shut in anticipation of the final heavy blow. The only fleeting thoughts were now those of happy horse riding capers with a beautiful girl, and of her warm lips resting upon his cheek. He was now sorry that he'd ever involved Megan in his quest, and if she was going to die, then that was what he wanted to do as well. So there he waited, and waited, and waited. Yet, even after what seemed like an age, no such strike arrived, and peering nervously back up to the man, Jason noticed that the weapon had been lowered.

The earl then replaced the blade into its cover and once again gazed threateningly into Jason's troubled face. 'I think it strange that my wife should die from a blow to the head, only to be followed by my daughter.' He slowly backed off. 'And yes…I should kill you here and now, but in the morning you shall be taken to the county gaol. And after the officials from the War Office have extracted what they can, you shall regret the day you were born.'

As the stable door was slammed closed, Jason was already thinking along similar lines, and in this wretched state he couldn't really care for what would happen to him next. Anyway, his parents would be just fine without him, he decided; his dad enjoying his never-ending pub lunch in Cockington, and his mum her perpetual spending spree in Oxford Street.

And so once more slumping back against the cold wall, Jason looked through the dusty skylight to the almost perfect lunar disc. The next day would be Belenos, and with it would arrive the blood moon and Ethera's accession. This was going to be the last time that the dell would witness such a special event, he now decided, and Jason was only sorry that he wouldn't be there.

Chapter Nine

Midsummer's day broke without ceremony. No singing, no dancing, no stones, no birthday cards; and within the apparently cosy confines of the stable, Jason shivered in the creeping early daylight. On a few occasions he'd been close to entering some sort of sleep, but the morning chill kept dragging him back to his painful reality. And with the rising sun filling the barn, he eventually opened his leaden eyelids to peer around.

Only one of the horses seemed to be alert, while the others, including George, stood dozing within their wooden stalls. Jason then looked up to the slates, beyond which he could hear a muffled dawn chorus. And in doing so, he became aware of something else – scraping sounds, as if a large bird had landed upon the roof and was losing its feet.

With the interior slowly emerging from its dusky gloom, he could now see an assortment of tools and equipment suspended from the walls and rafters. Some of them he recognised; a rake, a scythe, and a pitchfork. Other metallic implements he didn't, although he reckoned they wouldn't be out of place in a torture chamber.

One of the dusty skylights above the hayloft was propped open, allowing Jason to rest his aching eyes upon a slither of pale blue. If only he could free his wrists and feet he could climb up there and perhaps get to see Megan. However, his frantic attempt to do so was short lived, and stuck firmly behind his back Jason could only imagine how red-raw his wrists would have been from his efforts to escape. Now the pain was too intense to continue trying, and without any free hands he couldn't even begin on his other restraints.

There was nothing else for it. Once more he slumped against the icy wall, closed his eyes, and waited for the next part of his tortured journey. For soon, he knew that he would be on his way.

Allowing his thoughts to mingle with the cacophony of early morning birdsong, he began to glide into a semi-sleeping state. Before long, however, his efforts at nodding off were once again thwarted, not by the cold or pain, but by the unmistakable sound of metal dragging over stone. Jason hadn't heard anyone enter the stable, but for sure the earl had returned to fulfil his threat, and perhaps Megan's father now had in his hand one of those painful looking metal hooks that he'd seen earlier on the wall.

Jason was now beyond caring and just wanted it over with; whatever that may be. Then, finding the energy to raise his head, he came across the diffuse outline of someone in front of him. As he blinked a few times to clear his foggy vision, he saw that the figure carried a sword in one hand, with its point resting against the cobbles. But surely the earl was taller than this, he thought. And why should Megan's father now be standing with bare feet upon the cold ground?

Whoever it was remained silent and began to edge slowly nearer. Jason's heart began to pound, thinking that perhaps one of the stable lads had returned to give him a final going over before being passed on to the authorities. Then, as the character walked through a dusty beam of sunlight, Jason saw a face. His heart now missed a beat, realising that not too long ago this individual had wanted him dead.

The stocky figure then held a finger to his lips, before speaking in a quiet voice. 'Husht now. Us be here to get you out.'

Jason could now see the wart on the end of the elf's nose, but what did Div mean by *us*? Gazing up to the skylight, Jason discovered the answer. There, with his grinning face peering through the open skylight was Short, and he was holding a length of rope that ran into the hay store in the loft. Then looking once again to Div, Jason saw the elf produce a short knife from his belt, and very soon he had been released.

'What do you think you're doing?' was the teenager's immediate, whispered response. 'You could get yourself killed.'

'I'll tell you on the way back to the dell.' Div then took a firm hold of Jason's arm and pulled him to his feet. 'Because us be going...*now!*'

Initially, Jason readily complied with the order, but he soon paused at the bottom of the ladder that rose to the haymow. 'Sorry, but I can't leave here.' Then looking into the disbelieving eyes of his rescuer. 'Megan's been hurt bad, and I have to see her.'

'You be talking daft, lad.' The elf's voice rang with anger, and it was loud enough to startle a couple of the horses. Div described how Jason's rescue had been an order from Mans, and how under no circumstances were they to return without him. 'And even if I have to carry you there myself, I will. So get on up them steps.' The elf then brandished his sword in a threatening manner.

On the long walk back, the rescuers provided Jason with water and told him that a search party had been dispatched when he hadn't returned the previous night. He learned that his backpack had been found next to the waterfall, and that even in the bright moonlight the stream could be seen to run as red as Mans's robe. Yet, even as they offered their account, Jason's mind was elsewhere, and several times he pleaded with tears in his eyes to be allowed to return to see Megan.

'Listen,' said Div, eventually stopping and sounding irate. 'Once in the blooming hamlet you can do what you want, but until then you be going nowhere, lad.'

However, as the two woodlanders moved off, Jason did not follow.

'Sorry,' he said, 'but I *must* see Megan again. Even if she *is* dying.'

Div and Short each placed a hand upon their swords as if to encourage him to change his mind, but he had already calculated that they wouldn't do any harm.

'Please thank Mans for his efforts, and I'm sorry that I've failed him and the rest of the tribe.' Jason jogged off in the opposite direction towards the clearing, but he turned back for a brief moment and shouted: 'And tell Ethera and Tusher that I'll never forget them.'

Jason stood tall as he cut through the mist that clung to the clearing's dewy grass, and the way he felt, not even an army would stop him now. At first, the only other sign of life was the quarrelling magpies from the dell, but as he neared the manor he became aware of another commotion. Was it men shouting at one another? And if they were, they didn't sound too pleased.

Keeping to the middle of the clearing, Jason's pace was unerring and he held his head high. His view of the front of the manor may have been hazy, but nevertheless he saw three figures, and even from a distance he couldn't mistake the blurry outlines of the earl and the two stable lads. By now Jason could feel the sun warming his back, and moving closer he watched the men turn to confront him. Each of them raised a hand to shield their eyes from the dazzling morning rays, and their momentary inaction suggested that perhaps they couldn't believe what they were seeing.

Jason then noticed the earl gesture to the others, and within a moment Beckford and Ball had re-appeared carrying what looked like crossbows. Megan's father remained on the cobbles just in front of the columned entrance to the manor, and with his sword drawn he ordered his men to make the arrest.

'I don't knows how you done it, Frenchie' said Beckford, pointing his weapon into Jason's face, 'but you won't give us the slip again.'

After Jason was hauled to within a couple of paces from the earl, he stared into the man's bloodshot eyes and spoke in a measured tone. 'Please, Sir. I have returned to see Megan…if it's not too late.'

Her father frowned and walked forward to place the point of his sword under Jason's chin. 'And what sort of a person would have the temerity to return here to face certain death?'

Now with all three weapons trained upon him, Jason kept a straight face as he answered. 'Only someone who cares for your daughter and who isn't afraid of dying.' As quickly as he could, the teenager provided the story of how he came to be in the dell and of the plight of the Dumni. Then finishing with his own version of events surrounding Megan's injuries, a tear rolled down his bloodied cheek. 'So you see, I'm not a spy…and *definitely* not French.'

Following a long hesitation, the earl looked to the stable lads and then back to Jason. 'Do you really expect me to believe that you come from the future and that there are elves at large on my estate?'

Jason nodded. 'Megan told me that you believe the combe is haunted. Well, it's not like you think, but there's beings there who need you.'

The man appeared to consider Jason's words for a further short moment, before speaking in an angry tone.

167

'This is nothing but Devil talk. And you may not be French, but you shall now roast in hell for killing my daughter.'

Jason's legs almost buckled beneath him and his voice stuttered. 'Please…please tell me she's not…'

The earl stepped back and looked to the stable lads. 'Kill him now,' he ordered.

'With pleasure,' said Beckford.

'Aye,' echoed Ball, as they both took aim.

With eyes screwed tight, Jason waited for the fatal blows. However, after a long moment, no bolts came his way. Instead he heard music, or rather, singing. The words he recognised – and also the voice, complete with American accent.

'Just gimme respect, man. You know what I mean, Bro.

I ain't no sucker, no sucker for you, no…'

As Jason slowly opened his eyes, he could see the earl squinting past him and through the sunlight into the clearing that lay behind. Even the would-be executioners lowered their crossbows and stared in apparent disbelief at the two diminutive hooded figures moving in their direction through the misty strata. Except, one of them wasn't simply walking – it looked like he was dancing merrily towards the house.

Inwardly, Jason grinned. And he just *knew* that Tusher was in complete control when the elf stood next to him and nonchalantly said: 'Hey, man…what's going down?'

As Jason turned to see the elf boy's cheeky and smiling features, Ethera placed her hand upon his. Immediately, he was reassured and felt all his pain dissolve into her touch.

The earl shook his head and spoke to Jason in a stern manner. 'Only a complete coward would involve children in his dirty work.' He then turned to Tusher. 'Now, please be a good little boy and go back home to your mother.'

Jason saw the elf boy's face redden between the flashes of green paint, and he felt the need to step in. 'These are the people I was telling you about.'

'We are that,' added Ethera, who then lowered her hood, followed by Tusher.

Jason watched keenly as the earl and the stable lads fixed their wide eyes upon the elves' pointed ears.

''Tis a trick,' said Beckford, his voice shaking. 'Don't be fooled, M'Lord.'

'Aye,' said Ball, backing up his mate, but sounding equally uncertain. 'Either that, or these here be French for true.'

The anxiety etched upon the faces of Beckford and Ball had now transferred to the earl's, who edged closer to run his fingers over Ethera's ear. After a short moment he stepped back and said: 'This is Satan's work...kill them all.'

The earl lifted his blade and the stable lads their crossbows. However, just as they were about to act,

Ethera raised her pale hand and said: 'Before you slay us, I want you to listen to my friend.'

'Go on,' said the earl, still poised to strike. 'But make it quick.'

Tusher smiled before cupping his hands over his mouth and delivering the piercing blackbird distress call.

The silence that followed was broken only by the sardonic laughter from the earl. 'So the little wood sprite is casting a spell upon me, is he?'

'No…not me, Bro.' Now grinning, Tusher pointed over the towering crowns of the tree-lined dell. 'But them might.'

Emerging from the treetops, Jason saw what looked like a massive cloud of swarming crows; only, instead of cawing, the air was filled with ear-splitting yells. And as the dark shape loomed closer, he could see that the individual creatures within seemed more like giant buzzards, the likes of which he'd never seen before. After all, what bird of prey had arms, legs, and carried spears? Then, as the figures began to land upon the cobbles next to him, he felt the cool draught from their beating leathery wings. With his mouth wide, Jason turned to Tusher and slowly lifted up the back of the elf's green cloak. 'Why didn't you tell me?'

The elf boy said nothing, but simply smiled as the scene fell silent.

Beckford dropped his crossbow and raised his hands. ''Tis the last blooming time I be drinking that stuff.'

Ball did likewise, leaving the earl alone holding his sword. He looked fearful, but his tone was uncompromising.

'In the name of God I *order* you to get off my land,' he yelled at the large crowd.

Only some shuffles from within the mob disturbed the hush that ensued. Very soon the shifting crowd had formed a channel, which ran from the grass at the rear of the gathering up to the cobbled area at the front of the house. And not a word was uttered as Lus and Mans, in his royal regalia, strode along the elf-lined aisle.

The king stopped a few paces short of Megan's father. Reaching only to about the earl's lower chest, he looked up to the rooftop, chimneys, and surrounding trees, where an army with painted faces and loaded bows now inhabited all. He then turned to Jason.

'Can someone tell me what is going on here?' he demanded.

Ethera immediately stepped forward and spoke confidently. 'I shall soon be the leader of the tribe, and I thought the time right to act like one.' She went on to explain to her father that when Div and Short returned to the village empty-handed, they had been too afraid to approach him. She herself had then hastily organised this rescue attempt, saying that she had done so only because she thought that he would never have allowed anything so risky.

As the king gave his daughter a long, pensive look, Megan's father raised his sword and shouted. 'For the last time, I order you all to leave my land.'

Mans's eyes slowly swivelled around until they rested upon the earl's. 'And by what authority do you make such claims?'

'By that of King George,' came the indignant response.

Mans moved closer, his eyes bold and fixed. '*I* am the only king around here, and my people have lived in this dell since the dawn of time.'

The earl shook his head and sniggered. 'My daughter is gone, so it bothers me not that I should now die myself in defence of what is lawfully my own.' He then waved his sword around. 'So once more I shall tell you to leave, or be responsible for the spilling of more blood.'

At this moment Ethera stepped forward and introduced herself as the king's daughter. 'Please, good man that you are, your dear child is but asleep...I feel it.'

With moist eyes and a look of anguish, the earl slowly lowered his weapon, almost as though Ethera's gentle voice had touched a secret place within. 'No,' he said calmly. 'She breathed her last just after sunrise, and she now lies soulless in that room.' He pointed to the upper windows to the left of the doorway.

The elf girl then moved closer and reached out with her hand. 'Please, take me to her...*now*.'

As the earl contemplated the request, Jason also moved in. 'And me, *My Lord*.'

Following a long and tense delay, the earl nodded. 'Very well. I have nothing else to lose.' He then looked to Mans and pointed to the stable lads. 'And I ask that your people keep guard over these two until I find out the truth behind Megan's demise.'

The king agreed and ordered Lus to take charge of the situation.

Jason had walked through this front entrance before, but on this occasion he couldn't see any stained-glass window – only grey stone blocks. However, the spiral stairway was present, as was the huge bolted door.

With the earl leading, followed closely by Mans, Ethera, Tusher, and Jason, the group reached the top of the stone steps. They then veered right into the bleak corridor and stopped on the wooden floor outside the second door on their left.

'Be prepared,' said the earl shakily, before turning the handle on the door. 'For it is not a welcome sight.'

The heavy drapes blotted out virtually all the sunlight that would otherwise have graced the room, and the paltry flickers from a few candles did almost nothing to lift the gloom. One of these was sited on a small wooden table next to the head of a four-poster bed, and its glow only just managed to distinguish the vague and inert outline of someone lying under the covers with their head on the pillow.

'I did what I could,' said the earl, his face contorted with grief. 'But her injury was too severe.'

Tusher led Ethera over to the bedside, where she closed her eyes and stretched up to rest her hand upon Megan's body. 'All is not lost,' she said after a short time. 'But first, open the windows to allow the light of Belenos to come through. For I sense that darkness still fills this room.'

The earl proceeded to part the thick curtains and blow out the candles. Almost immediately Jason expressed a gasp at the sight before him – surely, this wasn't even the same person, he thought, as he leaned over her head upon the pillow. Where were her rosy features, her warm smile, and her flowing blonde locks? What had happened to her infectious giggle and her gentle, caring touch?

Jason placed a trembling hand upon the girl's frozen cheek. 'I'm sorry, Megan…really, I am.' And there he gazed at her for a long moment, sniffling, and wiping away his tears.

Eventually, Ethera put her hand on his. 'Please, Jason. Stand with the others and allow me to speak a while with her.'

As the elf girl stood next to the bed, her head only just reached the level at where Megan lay. And only after climbing up and kneeling next to the earl's daughter, was Ethera able to place her hands upon Megan's ghostly cheek. 'Your spirit may have departed from this body, but it has not yet passed into the other world.' She then positioned her own cheek upon Megan's and, closing her eyes, began to sing softly.

174

'My dear, my dear, where be thee my sweet.
An age, an age, since we last did meet.
So come ye back from yonder place,
For all to see your fair, fair face.'

Jason hadn't heard the words before, but the melody reminded him of the music to Greensleeves.

For some time Ethera continued to hum and sing. In doing so, she rocked gently to and fro whilst caressing Megan's ivory features, which were now bathed in bright sunlight.

Only very slowly did Jason become aware of the changes in Megan's appearance; so subtle, that they seemed not to have a beginning. Wasn't the dried blood around her lips disappearing, and likewise the matted red knots in her hair? Weren't her blonde locks beginning to glisten in the morning sun? And moving closer he also noticed a healthy rosy hue appearing on her cheeks and even some slight movement in the covers, as if she was breathing once again.

He wasn't alone in watching this transformation in Megan's appearance. Her father had also edged closer as Ethera applied her healing touch, and like Jason he stood speechless as the elf girl eventually slid off the bed to face them.

Ethera sighed deeply. 'Her body now lives, yet her spirit is not returned.' Then reaching out to hold Jason's trembling hand. 'The rest is up to you.'

For a moment he felt utterly confused. Just what could she mean?

The earl also seemed to have a problem in understanding what was going on. 'Are you saying that my daughter is alive?'

Ethera moved her hand into the earl's. 'Trust in me, and you shall be with her once again.'

Then, as crazy as it seemed, Jason's mind drifted back to some of the stories that he'd heard as a child and was struck with the obvious answer. Eventually, after forcing a deep breath, he faced Megan's father. 'Do you mind, My Lord, if I do what Ethera asks?'

After a short pause the earl placed a hand on the teenager's shoulder. 'Do what you must, young man.'

Jason sat on the edge of the bed and leaned over the girl's face. As he daintily stroked Megan's hair, he had long forgotten about the audience within the room; almost like he and she were the only two people left in the world. Nonetheless, the three words that he would breath as he closed his eyes and rested his cheek next to hers would remain shy of a whisper. And after doing so, he tenderly and briefly placed his lips upon Megan's.

Within a short moment Jason noticed a little movement in her eyelids. Not much, but enough to convince him that something was beginning to happen. The activity soon moved to her mouth, where she parted her lips and filled her lungs with the fresh morning air from a nearby open window. Megan even mumbled a few words and at the same time began to thrash around with her arms and legs. 'No…please. Leave him alone…'

With this, Jason immediately moved closer and gently squeezed her hand. 'I'm with you, my love.' These words seemed to calm Megan down, and soon she opened her eyes and turned her head to squint upon his face.

The Dumni stood in the background, as a smiling and tearful earl approached to place his hand upon those of his daughter and Jason. And there they remained in union for a long moment, until eventually Megan was helped to her feet.

At first she seemed surprised by the presence of the little people in her bedroom, but Jason decided that the time wasn't right for him to tell her of his exploits following her fall into the gorge – he would do so later. Instead, he helped her over to one of the large cushioned chairs where, following a drink of water, she was able to recount her own version of events within the dell.

After listening to her story, the earl placed his hand upon Jason's shoulder and begged forgiveness for the treatment that he'd received. He then walked over to the window and looked down at the multitude of woodlanders, some of which were still standing guard with spears at the ready next to Beckford and Ball.

After a short time he turned to the others within the room. 'On this glorious midsummer's day, let us all stand together in the beautiful morning air. For I have something to share with you.'

In stepping into the sunlight, the earl's first move was towards the stable lads. And as he approached, with

Megan close behind holding Jason's hand, the rough characters could be seen to squirm.

'Sorry, M'Lord,' said Beckford. '''Twas him who done...'

'*Enough.*' The blast from the earl repeated in echoes of echoes of echoes around the clearing. Then moving closer to the quaking figures. 'Go...and if I should ever see your ugly faces on this land again, I shall have you transported. *Do you understand?*'

The two men said nothing, each managing only a slight head movement.

'And don't go telling stories of pixies in the forest,' continued the earl, 'for no one in their right mind will ever believe the fanciful ravings of a pair of sots like you. Now go...and never return.'

The pair withdrew like skulking foxes and turned to run over the clearing, now and then slipping on their backsides in the dewy grass as they did so. Their comical departure precipitated loud bursts of laughter from the gathered crowd, and even the nearby magpies seemed to find things amusing.

As the uproar abated, a beaming earl held his radiant daughter by the hand and stood on the cobblestones outside the pillared entrance. Facing them were Mans, Ethera, Tusher, and Jason; with Lus and the rest of the crowd standing just behind.

Megan's father raised a hand to quell the last few murmurs, then began his address. 'For generations the Cockington family has lived in fear of the ghostly beings that were said to exist in this combe. Yet, in a strange sense, that forbidden valley seems to have a certain hold over those closest to me.' The earl gave a heartfelt account of how his own wife had dared to venture into the forest, only to be killed when she fell from her mount.

On hearing this, Jason began to understand Megan's obsession with horses, and why she felt so drawn to the dell.

The earl went on. 'But now, through your goodness and courage, you have returned something precious to me. And for that I shall be eternally grateful.' He smiled towards Jason and Ethera, before looking to Mans. 'And as we both lay claim to these lands, is it not proper that we should come together for the greater good?' The earl then held his hand out to the king. 'Do we have an agreement?'

Mans looked to the others in his party, all of whom were nodding enthusiastically, then offered his hand to Megan's father. 'From this day forth, let it be known that our land is your land, and your land is ours.' The spontaneous cheers reverberated around the clearing as the men came together.

Jason joined in the celebrations by lifting Megan off her feet and twirling her around, followed by Tusher, who did likewise with Ethera.

'*Please*, my good friends…' The earl was trying to speak again, and he succeeded only when all had settled down. 'It is only fitting that you should now invite me to your own dwelling place, for indeed it sounds wondrous.'

Mans smiled. 'Only if you have a zest for song and dance and merriment.'

As the scene once again descended into wild celebration, Jason felt Tusher take a tight grasp of his wrist, while Div clutched the other.

'What the…?' He had no time to offer any resistance and his stomach churned as he looked into Megan's startled face. He saw that Ethera was supporting one of her arms, with Short taking the other.

Tusher laughed and looked to Jason. 'Not everyone gets to travel like this.'

From Jason's new vantage point, the crowd below looked like an army of ants marching its way towards the dell. Then, looking over the forest, the sea of green seemed to meet with the still grey waters of Tor Bay and the rigging of the sailing ships within.

Together with Megan they soared high above the tallest trees and began an aerial tour of the dell. Jason soon recognised some of the landmarks; the main village, the open stretches of Dumni farmland, the Keeper's cottage, and lastly, the Great Circle – where he noticed that several groups of woodlanders had begun to congregate.

'Us be heading there now,' said Tusher, beginning to blow a little under the prolonged strain.

Megan and her escorts were the first to touch down on the rough grassland close to the circle. Her landing appeared to be gentle, unlike Jason's, after he was dropped from a little way off the ground.

Lying flat on his back, he looked up to the elf boy's smirking face. 'Sorry, mate,' he heard. 'Thought us was closer than that.' However, he didn't really mind that much and had been sure that, in the end, Tusher would get his own back for that kick in the shins.

Jason was soon standing hand in hand with Megan as the glade began to bustle with men, women, and children; all waiting their turn to thank the both of them for their bold efforts in securing a future for the tribe. He also noticed how they were all now dressed in elaborate colourful costumes and were adorned in ornate metallic and red-stoned jewellery.

He felt uneasy with the attention, claiming that nothing would have been possible without the help of Megan and the little people themselves. Nonetheless, along with his girlfriend, Jason accepted the many handshakes, waist high hugs, and pats on the back. The swelling numbers also brought with them a whole range of musical instruments, and soon they were producing an irregular combination of wind and strings and drums.

However, Jason knew that the players would soon be performing for real, as he watched the sun climb through a high ceiling of wispy cloud towards its solstice peak. And this now began to make sense to Jason; after all, why celebrate its rising at dawn?

Looking around, he saw other artists. Conjurers, jugglers and acrobats produced gasps and rapturous applause with their daring feats. Then more, sitting and holding captive their audience with romantic tales of ancient heroes, all of which somehow reminded him of the Cockington festival. The joyous atmosphere intensified as the morning progressed towards midday, by which time Jason noticed that a few of the men in the tribe appeared to be staggering. He had been offered some ale from a few slurring individuals but had declined, stating that he was too young to indulge. Even so, he still managed to join in with the celebrations until, under protest, Megan dragged him to his feet.

'Now I shall teach you to dance,' she insisted. 'And surely there is no more beautiful place than around this ancient circle.'

Jason immediately thought back to what he'd said in the car on the way to Cockington, and he could almost hear his father's sneering voice. *'What was that you said, Jaz, about never dancing around stones?'*

Safely away from parental ribbing, and after contending with the whoops from Tusher and his friends, Jason quickly relaxed and looked deeply into Megan's eyes.

'Now, just hold my hand and do as I say,' she said.

Jason listened closely to the instruction and stood face to face with her, with his right hand upon her lower back.

Megan then prompted him to perform a few simple steps and turns, and told him that this new type of dance in which partners were allowed to touch was the current fashion in Paris, but was still very much frowned upon in England.

It seemed to Jason like some sort of waltz, and he soon adopted a smoother and more fluid action. They then looped their way intimately around the Stone of Celest and were quickly followed by several others, dancing and singing merrily within the glade.

The two were still as one as they finally collapsed in fits of laughter onto the grass. Catching his breath, Jason then noticed the arrival of Mans and the earl, both sitting upon George's back.

After dismounting, the king led Megan's father to the central stone, before facing the large crowd. The scene quickly hushed, and Mans addressed his tribe. 'Myself and the earl have discussed much on our way to this sacred place, and we have now agreed on how best to move forward for our mutual benefit.'

He explained that the tribe would now assist the earl in maintaining the land and forest of his estate, as well as those of the dell. They would also provide food and clothing for the earl and his daughter. In return, the Dumni would be able to expand into new areas and grow more crops. Furthermore, the earl had also pledged to protect them from future generations of humans by the construction of a huge stone wall around the vulnerable stretches of the dell and a great part of the estate; a barrier so high and deep, that no man would ever pass.

Jason felt honoured that he would probably be the next human, other than Megan and her father, to set foot on

Dumni soil. It pleased him, too, that the loudly chuntering mass was beginning to nod in apparent agreement with the plan outlined by their king.

Mans once again asked for quiet, then continued. 'And now the sun fast approaches the zenith, so let us turn our eyes to the Stone of Celest and ask for the spirit of Belenos to descend upon us all.'

Jason watched as every one of the tribe, children included, shifted their attention to the central stone. He saw them gaze in silence at the grey protrusion, unmoving, as if waiting for something to arrive.

Almost immediately there came an intense burst of white light from the monolith, after which its carved surface produced a strange mixture of bright colours and swirling shapes. For a long moment these waxed and waned like a pulsating kaleidoscope, until the patterns evolved into familiar forms, which included bears, mammoths, and wolves.

At the same time, Jason looked up to see the blazing midday sun being tossed violently through the sky between the tails of the icy cirrus, before it slowly sank to become absorbed into the central stone.

With that, there appeared in the monolith a hazy image of a man with a long beard and dangling hooped earrings. Just what was *he* doing there? Jason almost called out, but before he could the vision had been replaced by another. Once again he recognised the individual; only, this time, the man had one red eye, one green, and carried a wooden staff. He then listened as the shimmering figure said: *'I am Belenos...light and life.'*

The sheer brilliance of the glare now pained Jason's eyes and forced him to turn his head to the side. Then using a hand for protection from the light, he saw that Megan, her father, and the Dumni were still gazing directly into the dazzling rock. They all seemed to be utterly spellbound by the occasion, just like in a trance, he thought. He even waved his hand for a moment in front of Megan's stricken face, but she remained unmoving.

Eventually, however, the sun re-emerged from the stone to return to its earlier position, and the radiation from the monolith diminished to a soft glow. Yet, with the exception of Jason and the robed character that had appeared close to the stone, everyone remained in a seemingly sleepy state.

Still pre-occupied and attempting to understand the surreal goings-on, he looked towards the old man. The Keeper's lips moved only to produce a wry smile. Even so, Jason heard a voice echo inside his head. *'Come by here, my friend.'*

Somehow he felt hypnotised by the man's words and found himself walking over without any conscious choice. And soon standing close to Bora, Jason began to quiz him about the events that he'd just witnessed.

'Any meaning is for you alone to discover,' said the Keeper.

Not surprised by the evasive response, Jason then looked to the others, who remained statuesque with their eyes still upon the stone. 'Tell me what you've done to them?' he demanded.

The Gatekeeper placed a hand on Jason's shoulder. 'Your obligations to these people have been met, and the time has come for you to return to your own world.'

For a short moment Jason was stunned into silence, and his features shone pale in the bright sunshine. 'But I...I want to stay here with Megan,' he eventually managed to squeeze past the choking lump he felt in his throat.

Bora shook his head and remained silent.

'But you said that no one would miss me, no matter how long I stayed,' Jason went on.

'And that is true,' the Keeper confirmed, 'but your continued presence here would undo the good you have achieved.' He then provided Jason with a short explanation of how any further actions in this period may adversely affect the future, and he reminded him of the historical facts that he'd already given to Megan; in particular, those surrounding the Napoleonic wars. The Keeper ended with a glaring frown.

'Well,' Jason replied, impishly. 'If you know everything, then that must be how it happened.'

Bora eventually grinned, then invited him to bid his farewells.

As Jason walked slowly over to Megan, the Keeper attempted to answer his earlier question. He explained that for her, along with all the others, time had ceased to exist after they had witnessed the initial pulse of searing light from the monolith, and that this state would prevail until Jason had returned to his own time.

And once again he pleaded with Bora to allow him to remain, but his words seemed to fall upon deaf pointed ears.

'For the Dumni to be truly saved, that cannot come to pass.'

'But will I ever see Megan again?' Jason sounded desperate and his eyes welled up.

The Keeper placed a hand upon Jason's and spoke solemnly. 'That is not for me to decide.'

With a tear beginning to roll down his cheek, Jason moved closer and gazed into her vacant eyes, which sparkled like pale emeralds in the sunlight. In this moment he longed for just one more dance, one more flight, and one more visit to the waterfall – but he knew that it wasn't to be. Lifting a hand, he tenderly stroked her face and ran his fingers through her wavy locks. 'I love you...and always will,' he said, before placing his lips upon Megan's rosy cheek.

His choking words were only just a whisper, yet even Bora's eyes had filled. Jason then went to share some time with Ethera, Tusher, Mans, and the earl. He even found a moment to give George a final pat on the neck.

The journey to the Keeper's cottage would take them through a now deserted hamlet, where Jason took a little time to assemble his belongings. Then looking around the empty settlement for a final time, he made a promise to himself that one day he would return.

On arrival at the Keeper's place, Bora opened the door and went in. Jason followed closely behind, and even though he'd shut his eyes in anticipation of some luminous event, the flash of light that he encountered was like a star exploding in his head.

Chapter Ten

Nearly a minute had passed before Jason was able to adjust his eyes to the near-blackness within the cottage, and he didn't even bother to ask the Keeper what was going on – he had already decided that he was alone. Then, hearing a car sound its horn in the distance, his heartbeat quickened.

Opening the creaky door and standing on the top step, he looked to the overhead stonework. The same few carved letters were visible between the ferns, but he now knew what lay hidden underneath. And there he saw it dance again; the little orange and brown butterfly that he'd seen on his initial visit to the old building.

Okay, first things first. What time was it? Jason produced the mobile phone from his jeans' pocket and turned it on to display **13.56**. Strangely, it seemed to him also like almost no time had elapsed since first visiting the cottage, and all that had passed in the dell hung by a fragile thread like a detaching dream. So once again he wondered if he'd simply fallen asleep or something.

Jason readily found the track that had led him to the Keeper's place only a few minutes earlier, it seemed, and he began the short walk back to the archway. Then passing the nearby lake, he noticed how much smaller it was once again and how the branches of the rhododendrons drooped into the still surface as they had done before.

With a growing sense of excitement, the priority now was to get out of here and tell his dad everything – even if he didn't want to listen. And by the time he passed through the arching portal and emerged into the clear sunshine on the other side he was almost sprinting.

Jason was pleased to find some transport parked in the lane, and out of breath he fell into the back seat. 'Where's the other horse and carriage; the one that brought me here?' he asked.

The young man holding the reins frowned and said: 'Sorry, but this is the only one.'

Jason slowly shook his head and laughed. 'I should have guessed, shouldn't I? Anyway, take me to the village centre, please. And *quick*.'

The coachman regarded him strangely. 'This isn't a charity, mate.' He then put out his hand. 'That'll be five pounds, if you don't mind.'

Jason eagerly handed over a ten-pound note, telling the man to keep the change. He then asked what day it was.

The coachman again looked at him oddly. 'It's Saturday, of course…midsummer's day.'

'Yes,' cried Jason, punching the air. He thanked the man, and for the next ten minutes he marvelled at the outstanding beauty of the passing countryside.

After jumping down from the carriage at the end of the journey, Jason dashed towards the inn. Then remembering something from earlier, he stopped and returned to the roadside close to the village map. For a few minutes he rummaged around amongst the bushes, before picking up his crushed fizzy drink can, which he now placed safely inside one of the bins.

Out of puff on entering the inn, he saw his dad at a nearby table and hastily walked over. Jason noticed that he'd just started his cheese ploughman's and was in deep conversation with a couple over the virtues of herbal remedies. Moving closer, the teenager listened for a moment, then offered his own expert advice on an effective treatment for arthritis. 'I think you'll find that if you crawl naked under some bramble vines when the moon is full, your problem will go.' Smirking, he looked to his dad.

'Thanks for that, Jaz. And by the look of things, you might just have done that yourself...only backwards.'

Jason glanced at his frayed and grubby clothing, and as his father went to continue with his meal and chat, he interrupted again, this time with some urgency. 'Sorry, but something's happened and I need to speak to you.'

His father frowned. 'Can't it wait for me to finish my meal?'

Jason said not, but he wouldn't be drawn any further until they were outside, for fear of anyone else hearing what he had to say.

Sighing, his dad placed the cutlery next to the granary bread on his plate and said goodbye to the couple. And after a quick slurp of beer he was soon sitting on a secluded bench, where his son began to rant about his recent exploits.

Occasionally, Jason would lower his voice if anyone ventured within earshot of his quick-fire account, and he was only too pleased that his dad allowed him to speak without asking any silly questions.

'...so what I want to do now is to get back in there. But this time, I want you to come with me to see for yourself.'

Now smiling, Dad moved closer to embrace his son. 'What a fantastic story...I'm so proud of you.'

Jason's face immediately lit up. 'So you believe me, then?'

Dad nodded. 'Of course, I do, Jaz. Cockington is awash with stories of little people hidden deep within the forest, and it seems to me that you've just given them a fighting chance.'

Jason's eyes opened wide and he clutched his father's arm. 'Well, in that case, what are we waiting for?'

However, with his smile quickly fading, Dad resisted the attempt to drag him along. 'Sorry, son. I can't go with you.'

Jason looked bemused. 'But why not?'

His dad paused for a moment, then said: 'It's like you say, Jaz. That wall was built to keep humans out, and I wouldn't like to interfere in a world full of the precious beings you describe.'

Jason groaned. 'Well, even if you won't come, I'm still going.'

'And why's that?'

'Because I need to know if the Dumni are still there, or if I just imagined it all.' The teenager's head dropped at this point, and Dad moved a hand to lift Jason's chin.

'And is there any other reason, son?' His words sounded sincere.

Jason slowly nodded, but said nothing. Then, with a determined look on his face he raced away, before turning round for a second to throw over his backpack. 'Look after this, Dad. And I'll see you back at that pub as soon as I can.'

Following a long run, Jason reached the spot where he'd previously crossed into the dell. The archway was still there, as was the rusting gate with its deterrent notice. However, judging by the tangled growth within the sturdy metal bars and the lack of any accessible path in the near-jungle on the other side, it seemed like nothing had passed through this way in years – not even time itself.

Jason proceeded to move slowly along a seemingly endless stretch of the towering wall, looking for any means by which to gain access, but every rock remained stuck fast. This barrier really had been built to last, he now realised. Then, just as he was on the brink of giving up, an idea came to mind. And why he hadn't thought of it before, Jason didn't know.

With renewed vigour he jogged back to the cricket field, where the crowd was beginning to dwindle in the late afternoon sun. And as he walked over the grass to catch his breath, Jason bent down to pick up a polystyrene food carton. It may not have been the one that he'd dropped earlier, but he still felt good as he placed it in one of the rubbish bins.

Soon he was standing next to the pillars at the entrance to the manor, waiting for his chance to slip inside. In the corner of his eye he thought that he saw a slight movement in the curtain of an upstairs window – but then nothing.

Following a couple of deep breaths, Jason opened the door and walked quietly along the corridor to pause under the stained-glass window. Now viewing things in much closer detail, the winged creatures that he'd seen before, he now recognised as Tusher and Ethera; both of them like birds on the wing gliding freely through the greenery. And on the forest floor, the two human figures gazing upwards, hand in hand, were unmistakable.

Jason stood wide-mouthed. The scene was so vivid that he could almost hear her tender voice and sense her warm hand in his. And once again becoming convinced that he *had* lived the dream, he managed to pull himself away and return to the large door underneath. Only now, it had no padlock attached, and with a clunk he slid the heavy bolt to one side.

The sight he met brought an immediate grin to his face. The doorway had opened out into a walled garden, beyond which loomed the ancient trees of the dell. The garden itself was packed with roses of different shades and scents, and the walls dripped in climbers. There was even a sundial at its centre and a few thoughtfully placed wooden benches.

A minute later, Jason had walked through the small arched gateway on the back wall and onto a forest trail. Looking around, he didn't see any familiar landmarks, but nonetheless he remained confident in his recently acquired woodland navigational skills.

Some time on, and after losing his bearings a couple of times, Jason eventually reached a clearing deep within the forest. As his heart raced, he then looked into the glade to find little thatched cottages with smoke rising from their chimneys. And although the village seemed a bit larger than it had been, he saw chickens and ducks roaming freely around the central area and knew that he was at the right place.

'Hello,' Jason cried out, trying to control his growing excitement. 'Is there anybody here?'

After receiving nothing but a few clucks in return, he strolled through the village, where he even paid a visit to Mans's cottage. On finding the whole hamlet deserted, Jason was left scratching his head, attempting to figure out what was going on – until a minute later he felt like kicking himself. After all, where should he have expected the tribe to be on midsummer's day?

Nearing his next destination, Jason was again perturbed with the apparent lack of activity. From his location on the forest trail he didn't expect to see anything through the thick foliage, but if the Dumni were in the vicinity, surely by now he would have heard something of their wild solstice celebrations.

Then, as he eventually reached the clearing that contained the monolith, the scene that emerged astounded him. How could so many people create so little noise? More than that, how could such a huge crowd possibly maintain this complete silence? Could it be that they were in a trance, just like he'd left them before?

Moving closer, Jason noticed that they were dressed once again in flamboyant fashion, wearing hats, jewellery, and coloured robes as they had been at the feast of Belenos. Some of them also carried drums, and fiddles, and whistles.

Soon there came a sound from within the gathering, as if a single person had begun a slow handclap. Then another, and another.

Walking on regardless, Jason heard the noise escalate into one of rapturous applause; so intense that he almost had to put his hands to his ears. The standing ovation continued as some of the little people then scampered over the rough grass to greet him.

Eventually, one of the older figures barged to the front of the welcoming party and offered his hand. 'Remember me?'

The real giveaway was the wart on the end of the man's nose. Jason moved closer and crouched down to embrace him. 'Hello, Div, my old friend. How are you?'

'Just proper,' came the reply. 'And you ain't changed a bit...not even they clothes.'

The crowd seemed to find this amusing, and soon a tearful Jason was strolling around, smiling broadly, and meeting people that he hadn't seen for several hours, although he did appreciate that things would seem somewhat different for them. Before long, however, he was asking over the whereabouts of certain others that appeared to be missing.

'Mans be resting yonder,' said Short, arriving on the scene and pointing to one of the dark headstones encircling the monolith. He went on to describe how Bora hadn't been sighted since the night Ethera had become queen – the very same day as Jason himself was seen to dissolve into the monolith's brilliant light. 'And as for Tush...' The stocky character looked directly into the setting sun, from where three figures were approaching.

Jason shaded his eyes with a hand, and he felt his pulse bound faster and faster. Then, as the trio stopped next to him, he looked to the faces of the man, woman, and boy. These were people that he'd seen before; the singing coachman, along with his hooded companion, and the assistant from Weaver's Cottage Tea Shoppe.

'Welcome back, Jason,' said the woman, looking through his face with her hazy blue eyes.

And within her gaze, distant but clear, Jason saw a young elf girl; one with healing powers and who had saved his life – not once, but twice. She now wore the studded Moon Cross that he'd last seen around her father's neck, and with a tear in his eye Jason bowed before the queen. 'It's great to see you all again, Ethera. And sorry I couldn't say a proper goodbye last time.'

Tusher then joined in. 'Only glad you made it, mate…but just keep them muckle feet to yourself.' He finished with a smile, and along with Ethera gave Jason a long hug.

The sun had set by the time Jason heard of their marriage and been introduced to their son, Lans. He was then told that the blood moon was only a matter of hours away, and that the boy was soon to become King of the Dumni.

'And even though we have heard nothing from the Keeper in over two centuries,' said Ethera, 'we have known – through what you told us all those years ago – that the magical event would take place this very evening.'

Musical notes then began to drift through the clearing, and the smoke from scores of newly lit torches belched into the dusky air. Jason hadn't been surprised to meet up with some of his old friends again; after all, they *were* a long-lived race. However, the question he had been avoiding could wait no longer, and he tentatively enquired over Megan.

After doing so, the music suddenly stopped. And as Jason glanced around to figure out what was going on, Ethera came to hold his hand. She began to tell him of a tale that had been recounted around the tribal fires for the past two hundred or so years, and she spoke of a maid who was heartbroken following the disappearance of her lover from the Great Circle at the feast of Belenos.

Jason then heard how, in her despair, the girl had pleaded with her father to be allowed to visit the Gatekeeper, and to ask Bora Macool for passage into her lover's world.

'Eventually, after a few weeks, her father agreed,' Ethera went on. 'And the story ends with her setting off early one misty morning on her favourite horse to ride to the Keeper's place, never to be seen again.'

Jason shook his head. 'You mean Megan just vanished into thin air?'

'Yeah, she did, Jaz. Just like you.'

Jason couldn't believe the voice that he'd just heard and quickly spun round. He then watched as the crowd parted to leave two bearded figures standing alone at the end of the elf-lined pathway. They stood much taller than the others did, and as they walked closer Jason could see that the older of the two men had pigtails and wore a long white robe, adorned with stars and crescent moons. He soon recognised him as the elusive character that he'd met when browsing through the second-hand bookstall at the Cockington festival. He then turned his attention to the individual walking alongside. This one wore a waistcoat, a feathered fedora, and golden hooped earrings. The pair ambled to a rest just a few paces short of Jason, who by now was standing with a bewildered look on his face.

'Thought I should join you, Jaz,' said the man in the waistcoat.

Jason eventually found his tongue. 'But how…?'

His dad placed a hand upon Jason's shoulder. 'It's a long story, son.'

'But…you two know each other?' Jason stuttered

'Yeah. This is Steve. I do his garden and we play in a band together.' Then grinning. 'He's also the present day Earl of Cockington.'

Jason learned how his dad had helped this man to stage the Cockington festival in the first place, and that his own visit to the event had been planned for quite some time.

'So what are you?' he asked, turning to the robed figure and sounding a little irate. 'The fifteenth earl, or the sixteenth, or something?'

'No,' said the man, smiling. 'I am the tenth. And before I forget…the War Office asked me to thank you for telling us about Trafalgar and Waterloo.'

The crowd remained hushed as Jason again struggled to find his words. 'But you can't…I mean…when I was here before I met the tenth earl and I…' Looking beyond the man's grey beard and weathered creases, there began to emerge the face of a person who had once held a sword to his throat, only much older. He also recalled that Megan's father was called Stephen. 'But that's impo…'

Just then, through the cool twilight air, Jason heard the distant but distinct plodding of hooves – and his heart skipped a beat. At the end of the same newly formed channel from where his dad and the earl had first appeared, he saw someone sitting upon a huge white horse, facing forward, and with both booted legs to one side. Only now, the walls of elves held aloft their burning torches to form what looked like a flickering guard of honour. Feeling his chest tighten, Jason also began to experience an inward rush that had been absent since the time at the waterfall. Okay, Jaz. Just stay cool. Deep breath in…and out, and in…and out.

Step by slow step the horse drew ever closer, and Jason realised that he'd encountered this animal before. Not only was this the great beast that he'd ridden over Chelston meadow two hundred odd years ago; it was also the one that pulled the carriage that had taken him to the Keeper's cottage earlier that day.

Looking to the saddle, Jason noticed the flowery crown upon the rider's blond hair and her shimmering green velvet outfit. His eyes then rested upon the girl's radiant smile, and he only just managed to take a couple of shaky steps forward. 'But this can't be…' he mumbled.

The horse stopped next to Jason and, as Megan slid from the saddle and into his waiting arms, he stared into the young rider's ageless features.

'I love you, Jason.' The girl's tear-filled eyes glistened in the torchlight. 'And I always have.'

Cheering and clapping and dancing accompanied the embrace that followed, and for a long moment Jason and

Megan held one another, and whispered, and loved, just like dreamy newly-weds.

Their fathers and friends then joined the intimate young couple and, as they all sat on the grass, Jason was given a history of events.

He learned that Megan had re-appeared in the dell with George just after sunrise on the morning of the Cockington festival; apparently, just as everyone had hoped. Also, he was told that the monolith's mesmerising light, generated each feast of Belenos at midday, was held responsible for the tribe's longevity – and for that bestowed upon Megan's father.

From within his robe the earl then produced a faded, red cloth-bound book. 'This is the fantasy tale I was telling you about; one given to me a long time ago for safekeeping.' He handed it to Jason, who looked to the handwritten gilt lettering of the title.

'Well, it certainly is that,' Jason said. He then moved his eyes to the bottom of the front cover and noticed the author's name.

Turning to Megan, he heard how, in an attempt to cope with her grief, she had decided to write of their days together and of the young man who had saved a tribe of elves in the forest around Cockington.

'...and as you can see,' she continued, 'it ends with our hero disappearing into the light from the Stone of Celest.' She then snuggled closer to Jason. 'And at long last, you can now help me to complete my book, and to give it the satisfactory ending that such a tale requires.'

Both fathers eventually left their children to get on with things, saying that they were going to perform with the other musicians. And for some time Jason and Megan remained inseparable on the grass, whilst the rising full moon illuminated the glade with its silvery rays.

Soon, however, with the chanting and dancing and storytelling in full flow, the ambient light began to change. And as it did so, all festive activity came to grinding halt.

One small corner of the earth's heavenly partner had turned a dusky red, as had the headstones around the central stone. With the silence prevailing, all eyes were now fixed upon the helpless celestial body as it was overrun by a creeping fiery hue, and very soon the process was complete, precipitating a few whoops and gasps from the audience far below. For a short time after, the blood moon weaved a merry dance through the ribbon of the Milky Way, before appearing to descend into the monolith.

To begin with, the Stone of Celest adopted the same red colour, but very quickly it brightened into a towering blaze, throwing out tongues of fire in all directions to the surrounding headstones, which began to rotate rapidly like a gigantic Catherine wheel. All at once everyone seemed to cower from the searing intensity of the event, and only when Jason felt the heat easing to something more tolerable, was he brave enough to return his eyes to the central stone.

With the moon now restored to the night sky, the monolith had reverted to a soft reddish glow. All the flaming activity had ceased, and Jason could see thick smoke hanging in the air around the Great Circle, but strangely, he detected no burning smell.

Only as the scene cleared, did he begin to notice the group of robed figures standing where once the headstones had. And looking closer, even in the restricted light of the elves' burning torches, Jason recognised two of the men.

An older looking Mans stood closest and, like most of the others, was dressed in regal red. The one exception, carrying a staff and wearing a robe of brown and orange, seemed not to have aged at all. The Gatekeeper then walked over to the congregated Dumni, where there had appeared a wooden chair, just like the one Jason had seen in Bora's cottage.

No one yet dared to speak, it seemed, and Jason clutched Megan's hand as Ethera and her son approached the decorative piece of furniture.

Reaching the Keeper, the queen bowed her head and allowed the removal of the Moon Cross. It was then placed by Bora around the slender neck of Lans, who was ushered into his throne, whilst everyone else fell on one knee. And as soon as the new monarch had taken his place, the onlooking ancestors appeared to dissolve into the night air, leaving behind only the circle of headstones.

After this, the Keeper walked over to where the teenagers were standing, and he looked into Jason's eyes. 'I see a young man where once there was a boy.' Then turning to Megan. 'And I just know that you will look after one another in your old age.'

Megan thanked the Gatekeeper for what he'd done for her and her father, and she stooped to land a kiss on his cheek. 'You never expected that, did you?' she said, smiling.

Bora blushed, and he seemed to be stuck for words for a moment. 'Well, er, I suppose even omniscient beings can have an off day.' Grinning, the Keeper winked at the pair with his shining green eye and crashed his staff to the ground, sending a glittering shower of dust over them.

With the white moonlight once again beginning to flood the scene, Bora turned to the others and asked them to stand. 'Let us now celebrate with our new king.' And after saying so, he melted into the jubilant crowd.

Within the joyous melee Jason looked to Megan and tidied the crown of marguerites on her head. 'So what's the chance of another one of those dances?' he asked, his eyes begging.

The girl smiled; cheekily, thought Jason, before she began to back away. 'Fair, but you shall have to catch me first...'

The party continued until the voices and legs and bellies could take no more. And in the first light of dawn, Jason bade farewell to the king and his tribe and promised to visit them as often as he could.

At the earl's invitation, Jason and his dad would rest the next few hours in the manor house. Reaching the grand old building, the two older men went to the drawing room, where they began to reflect on the day's events.

After settling George into the stables, Jason and Megan made their way to a chaise longue within the entrance hallway where, in the presence of the stained-glass window, they exchanged their own adventures. And there they bragged and laughed and preened and teased, until eventually Jason felt Megan's head resting upon his shoulder.

The daylight was now streaming through the imposing window, and its inherent characters seemed to dance along to the distant sound of birdsong from somewhere outside the building. Then, as he laid Megan's drowsy head upon his lap, Jason's own eyelids began to drop, and he couldn't quite work out when he'd last slept. Was it the previous night at his mother's house in Exeter, or over two hundred years ago in the dell? It felt like the latter.

Still trying to decide for sure, something else came to mind. Sliding his fingers inside his jeans' pocket, Jason came across what felt like the collection of worry dolls. Smiling, he couldn't think of anything that was now bothering him; things couldn't get much better, it seemed. Nonetheless, they would come in handy one day, he reckoned.

Then, just as Jason felt himself drift away, he became aware of a man's voice coming from the large door that had earlier led into the walled garden.

'Sleep now, my son. For you have served me well.'

Barely able to lift his eyelids, Jason squinted towards the doorway, which then silently swung open. Could it have been his fatigued mind playing tricks, or was his dad really standing there, gazing upon him with one red eye and one green?

With his skin prickling, Jason turned away for a brief moment. However, when he looked back, his only hazy view was that of a small orange and brown butterfly that danced around the opening, before disappearing into one of the rose beds.

(Pyronia tithonus)

Hedge Brown

Also known as The Gatekeeper